W9-AYN-396

THE ANNOTATED SHAKESPEARE

# The Merchant of Venice

## William Shakespeare

*Fully annotated, with an Introduction, by Burton Raffel*

*With an essay by Harold Bloom*

THE ANNOTATED SHAKESPEARE

*Yale University Press* • *New Haven and London*

Excerpt from Harold Bloom's Modern Critical Interpretations,
*William Shakespeare's The Merchant of Venice,* copyright © 1986,
reprinted with permission of Chelsea House Publishers,
a subsidiary of Haights Cross Communications.

Designed by Rebecca Gibb.
Set in Bembo type by The Composing Room of Michigan, Inc.
Printed in the United States of America by R. R. Donnelley & Sons.

Library of Congress Cataloging-in-Publication Data
Shakespeare, William, 1564–1616.
The Merchant of Venice / William Shakespeare ; fully annotated,
with an introduction, by Burton Raffel ; with an essay by Harold Bloom.
      p.     cm. — (The annotated Shakespeare)
Includes bibliographical references.
ISBN-13: 978-0-300-11564-2 (paperbound)
ISBN-10: 0-300-11564-4 (paperbound)
1. Jews—Italy—Drama.   2. Venice (Italy)—Drama.
3. Moneylenders—Drama.   I. Raffel, Burton.   II. Bloom, Harold.
III. Title.
PR2825.A2R34 2006
822.3′3—dc22
2006005490

A catalogue record for this book is available from the British Library.

10 9 8 7 6 5 4 3 2 1

To the memory of my father, my mother,
my brother, and all the others

# CONTENTS

The learnèd doctor of the law, Belario, is never seen or heard on stage. But the chief judge, the Duke of Venice, reads aloud a letter from Belario:

*Duke* Meantime the court shall hear Belario's letter: (*reading aloud*) "Your Grace shall understand, that at the receipt of your letter I am very sick, but in the instant that your messenger came, in loving visitation was with me a young Doctor of Rome, his name is Balthasar. I acquainted him with the cause in controversy between the Jew and Antonio the merchant. We turned o'er many books together. He is furnished with my opinion, which bettered with his own learning (the greatness whereof I cannot enough commend), comes with him at my importunity to fill up your Grace's request in my stead. I beseech you, let his lack of years be no impediment to let him lack a reverend estimation, for I never knew so young a body with so old a head. I leave him to your gracious acceptance, whose trial shall better publish his commendation."

This was perfectly understandable, we must assume, to the mostly very average persons who paid to watch Elizabethan plays. But though much remains clear, who today can make full or entirely comfortable sense of it? In this very fully annotated edition, I therefore present this passage, not in the bare form quoted above, but thoroughly supported by bottom-of-the-page notes:

*Duke* Meantime the court shall hear Belario's letter:
(*reading aloud*)[1] "Your Grace shall understand, that at the
receipt of your letter I am[2] very sick, but in the instant
that your messenger came, in loving visitation was with
me a young doctor[3] of Rome, his name is Balthasar. I acquainted him with the cause[4] in controversy between the
Jew and Antonio the merchant. We turned o'er[5] many
books together. He is furnished with my opinion, which
bettered[6] with his own learning (the greatness whereof
I cannot enough commend), comes[7] with him at my importunity[8] to fill up your Grace's request in my stead.[9]
I beseech you, let his lack of years be no impediment to
let him lack a reverend[10] estimation, for I never knew so
young a body with so old a head. I leave him to your gra-

---

1 it is not clear whether it is the Duke or a court official who reads the letter
  aloud
2 was
3 lawyer
4 case, action*
5 turned over = read through, searched, perused
6 improved
7 i.e., Belario's opinion comes
8 solicitation, urging
9 (it is not clear exactly what the Duke has requested of Belario)
10 respectful, courteous

cious acceptance, whose trial[11] shall better publish[12] his commendation."

Without full explanation of words that have over the years shifted in meaning, and usages that have been altered, neither the modern reader nor the modern listener is likely to be equipped for anything like full comprehension.

I believe annotations of this sort create the necessary bridges, from Shakespeare's four-centuries-old English across to ours. Some readers, to be sure, will be able to comprehend unusual, historically different meanings without any glosses. Those not familiar with the modern meaning of particular words will easily find clear, simple definitions in any modern dictionary. But most readers are not likely to understand Shakespeare's intended meaning, absent such glosses as I here offer.

My annotation practices have followed the same principles used in *The Annotated Milton,* published in 1999, and in my annotated editions of *Hamlet,* published (as the initial volume in this series) in 2003, *Romeo and Juliet* (published in 2004), and subsequent volumes in this series. Classroom experience has validated these editions. Classes of mixed upper-level undergraduates and graduate students have more quickly and thoroughly transcended language barriers than ever before. This allows the teacher, or a general reader without a teacher, to move more promptly and confidently to the nonlinguistic matters that have made Shakespeare and Milton great and important poets.

It is the inevitable forces of linguistic change, operant in all liv-

---

11 putting to the proof, testing ("performance")
12 declare

ing tongues, which have inevitably created such wide degrees of obstacles to ready comprehension—not only sharply different meanings, but subtle, partial shifts in meaning that allow us to think we understand when, alas, we do not. Speakers of related languages like Dutch and German also experience this shifting of the linguistic ground. Like early Modern English (ca. 1600) and the Modern English now current, those languages are too close for those who know only one language, and not the other, to be readily able always to recognize what they correctly understand and what they do not. When, for example, a speaker of Dutch says, "Men kofer is kapot," a speaker of German will know that something belonging to the Dutchman is broken ("kapot" = "kaputt" in German, and "men" = "mein"). But without more linguistic awareness than the average person is apt to have, the German speaker will not identify "kofer" ("trunk" in Dutch) with "Körper"—a modern German word meaning "physique, build, body." The closest word to "kofer" in modern German, indeed, is "Scrankkoffer," which is too large a leap for ready comprehension. Speakers of different Romance languages (French, Spanish, Italian), and all other related but not identical tongues, all experience these difficulties, as well as the difficulty of understanding a text written in their own language five, or six, or seven hundred years earlier. Shakespeare's English is not yet so old that it requires, like many historical texts in French and German, or like Old English texts—for example, *Beowulf*—a modern translation. Much poetry evaporates in translation: language is immensely particular. The sheer *sound* of Dante in thirteenth-century Italian is profoundly worth preserving. So too is the sound of Shakespeare.

I have annotated prosody (metrics) only when it seemed

truly necessary or particularly helpful. Readers should have no problem with the silent "e" in past participles (loved, returned, missed). Except in the few instances where modern usage syllabifies the "e," whenever an "e" in Shakespeare is *not* silent, it is marked "è." The notation used for prosody, which is also used in the explanation of Elizabethan pronunciation, follows the extremely simple form of my *From Stress to Stress: An Autobiography of English Prosody* (see "Further Reading," near the end of this book). Syllables with metrical stress are capitalized; all other syllables are in lowercase letters. I have managed to employ normalized Elizabethan spellings, in most indications of pronunciation, but I have sometimes been obliged to deviate, in the higher interest of being understood.

I have annotated, as well, a limited number of such other matters, sometimes of interpretation, sometimes of general or historical relevance, as have seemed to me seriously worthy of inclusion. These annotations have been most carefully restricted: this is not intended to be a book of literary commentary. It is for that reason that the glossing of metaphors has been severely restricted. There is almost literally no end to discussion and/or analysis of metaphor, especially in Shakespeare. To yield to temptation might well be to double or triple the size of this book—and would also change it from a historically oriented language guide to a work of an unsteadily mixed nature. In the process, I believe, neither language nor literature would be well or clearly served.

Where it seemed useful, and not obstructive of important textual matters, I have modernized spelling, including capitalization. Spelling is not on the whole a basic issue, but punctuation and lineation must be given high respect. The Quarto uses few exclamation marks or semicolons, which is to be sure a matter of the conventions of a very different era. Still, our modern preferences cannot be lightly substituted for what is, after a fashion, the closest thing to a Shakespeare manuscript we are likely ever to have. We do not know whether these particular seventeenth-century printers, like most of that time, were responsible for question marks, commas, periods, and, especially, all-purpose colons, or whether these particular printers tried to follow their handwritten sources. Nor do we know if those sources, or what part thereof, might have been in Shakespeare's own hand. But in spite of these equivocations and uncertainties, it remains true that, to a very considerable extent, punctuation tends to result from just how the mind responsible for that punctuating *hears* the text. And twenty-first-century minds have no business, in such matters, overruling seventeenth-century ones. Whoever the compositors were, they were more or less Shakespeare's contemporaries, and we are not.

Accordingly, when the original printed text uses a comma, we are being signaled that *they* (whoever "they" were) heard the text, not coming to a syntactic stop, but continuing to some later stopping point. To replace commas with editorial periods is thus risky and on the whole an undesirable practice. (The dramatic action of a tragedy, to be sure, may require us, for twenty-first-century readers, to highlight what four-hundred-year-old punctuation standards may not make clear—and may even, at times, misrepresent.)

When the printed text has a colon, what we are being signaled is that *they* heard a syntactic stop—though not necessarily or even usually the particular kind of syntactic stop we associate, today, with the colon. It is therefore inappropriate to substitute editorial commas for original colons. It is also inappropriate to employ editorial colons when *their* syntactic usage of colons does not match ours. In general, the closest thing to *their* syntactic sense of the colon is our (and their) period.

The printed interrogation (question) marks, too, merit extremely respectful handling. In particular, editorial exclamation marks should very rarely be substituted for interrogation marks.

It follows from these considerations that the movement and sometimes the meaning of what we must take to be Shakespeare's play will at times be different, depending on whose punctuation we follow, *theirs* or our own. I have tried, here, to use the printed seventeenth-century text as a guide to both *hearing* and *understanding* what Shakespeare wrote.

Since the original printed texts (there not being, as there never are for Shakespeare, any surviving manuscripts) are frequently careless as well as self-contradictory, I have been relatively free with the wording of stage directions—and in some cases have added brief directions, to indicate who is speaking to whom. I have made no emendations; I have necessarily been obliged to make choices. Textual decisions have been annotated when the differences between or among the original printed texts seem either marked or of unusual interest.

In the interests of compactness and brevity, I have employed in my annotations (as consistently as I am able) a number of stylistic and typographical devices:

- The annotation of a single word does not repeat that word
- The annotation of more than one word repeats the words being annotated, which are followed by an equals sign and then by the annotation; the footnote number in the text is placed after the last of the words being annotated
- In annotations of a single word, alternative meanings are

usually separated by commas; if there are distinctly different ranges of meaning, the annotations are separated by arabic numerals inside parentheses—(1), (2), and so on; in more complexly worded annotations, alternative meanings expressed by a single word are linked by a forward slash, or solidus: /

- Explanations of textual meaning are not in parentheses; comments about textual meaning are

- Except for proper nouns, the word at the beginning of all annotations is in lower case

- Uncertainties are followed by a question mark, set in parentheses: (?)

- When particularly relevant, "translations" into twenty-first-century English have been added, in parentheses

- Annotations of repeated words are *not* repeated. Explanations of the *first* instance of such common words are followed by the sign ★. Readers may easily track down the first annotation, using the brief Finding List at the back of the book. Words with entirely separate meanings are annotated *only* for meanings no longer current in Modern English.

*The most important typographical device here employed is the sign ★ placed after the first (and only) annotation of words and phrases occurring more than once. There is an alphabetically arranged listing of such words and phrases in the Finding List at the back of the book. The Finding List contains no annotations but simply gives the words or phrases themselves and the numbers of the relevant act, the scene within that act, and the foot-note number within that scene for the word's first occurrence.*

Written in the period 1596–1598, *The Merchant of Venice* was first printed in 1600. This quarto-sized book, which has become the basic text for all modern editions, also gives us, directly and immediately via the volume's title page, a good idea of what the printer-publisher thought was most worthy of public attention. "The most excellent history of the Merchant of Venice, with the extreme cruelty of Shylock the Jew towards the said merchant, in cutting a just pound of his flesh, and the obtaining of Portia by the choice of three chests."[1] The Quarto text is so clean that scholars think it was quite probably printed directly from Shakespeare's manuscript. Whether or not Shakespeare had anything to do with the title page (most likely he did not), the description of the play focuses on three plot lines: first, Antonio the merchant of Venice; second, Shylock, the rapacious, almost fiendish Jewish moneylender; and third, the courting—by an odd sort of lottery-like procedure—and winning of Portia, a singularly wealthy young heiress. Note that the most intensely dramatic portion of the description is that concerning Shylock, who has often been mistakenly thought of as the "merchant" of the play's title. The writer of the title page plainly saw Shylock's part of the narrative as the play's best selling aspect.

As is so often the case with Shakespeare, many elements of the story are borrowed, in this case principally from *Il Pecorone* ("The Blockhead"), a collection of stories published in Florence in 1558 and not at that time translated into English. It has been argued, sensibly and on the basis of the totality of Shakespeare's work, that he could read Italian. The details of the original tale are of some interest, but will not be here discussed: what is most relevant to readers of this edition is how Shakespeare presents material from all his sources, and thus how it seems most accurately and usefully to read his play as we have it.

*The Merchant of Venice* comes early in what might be called Shakespeare's "middle" period, shortly after *Romeo and Juliet* and *A Midsummer Night's Dream* and just before *Henry the Fourth, Part One*. The play features a good deal of the "low" comedy to be seen in *The Taming of the Shrew*, which dates from roughly four years earlier. There is also, in the more "serious" parts of the play (those in verse rather than in prose), some of the most beautifully worked-out passages Shakespeare ever wrote:

Your mind is tossing on the ocean,
There where your argosies with portly sail
Like signiors and rich burghers on the flood,
Or as it were the pageants of the sea,
Do overpeer the petty traffickers
That curtsy to them, do them reverence,
As they fly by them with their woven wings.

(1.1.7–13)

Spoken by one the minor characters, Salarino, about the merchant Antonio, these seven lines are composed of a single tightly woven sea-metaphor. The passage traces Antonio's state of mind, subtly employing the nature of his profession to give us two trains of thought at the same time: the preoccupations of Antonio's mind, and the preoccupations of his business. The passage is also a bold proclamation of the poet-playwright's superb literary mastery. We do not need to know who or what Shakespeare was, nor do we need to understand every one of these lines in detail, to realize that we have here been launched on a tautly controlled literary-dramatic expedition.

But just as there are necessary limitations to our ability to understand all of Shakespeare's *words,* so too there are broader aspects of the play that are historically conditioned and not fully comprehensible without explanation. In matters of religious belief, even matters of knowledge, *The Merchant of Venice* must be approached, today, with caution. We know little about Shakespeare's life (though more than enough to have no doubt that he wrote his plays). We know virtually nothing about his likes and dislikes, or (though he may sometimes seem to know everything knowable) the true extent of his knowledge. He must have enjoyed success, or he would hardly have worked so intensely at achieving it. He used his money to buy land, and to purchase a coat of arms. But who does not enjoy success? Who in a land-dominated culture does not value its ownership? Who in a fiercely status-conscious society does not desire a degree of status?

We must be particularly careful not to lean on a tremendously effective and enormously popular comic drama, trying to place it in an ideological schema—like that which we have come to call anti-Semitism—in which it has little if any legitimate place.

Shakespeare surely shared much of the experience common to most Elizabethans. But though incredibly gifted, he remains no more than human. Most of the people he knew were Christian, and he had to know a good deal about that faith. Did he know any Muslims, and what did he know about Islam? There is a total lack of evidence. But did he know any Jews, and what did he know about Judaism? The play plainly seems to be deeply concerned with both Jews and Judaism; Shylock and his daughter are major players in the plot. But what is the true role and importance of their stated religious identity? How much are either Jews or Judaism the play's concerns?

*The Merchant of Venice* is dramatic fiction, and fiction is by definition pretense: the writer tries (and Shakespeare brilliantly succeeds) in making us believe in his fiction. The writer (and even more, the good writer) rarely has much interest in persuading us that his fiction is fact. No matter how devoted he or she may be to a cause or to a belief system, it is the fiction that matters the most—to the writer as to us. When we learn that in fact, despite an ancient expulsion of the Jews, "there were Jews in Shakespeare's England," what have we learned about Shakespeare's play? When we are told, further, that the number of such Jews was "probably never more than a couple of hundred at any given time," have we any useful information about either Shakespeare or his play?[2] On the other hand, knowing that "a villainous Jewish usurer was being portrayed on the London stage some twenty years before *The Merchant of Venice* was written" seems decidedly relevant, for this helps us understand the background from which the play emerged.[3] Similarly, it is useful to know that "England's fascination with the conversion of the Jews had begun in earnest in the late 1570s and early 1580s and was quite well established by the time that Shakespeare wrote *The Merchant of Venice*."[4]

James Shapiro, who has made a thorough study of the matter, explains that "the word *Jew* had entered into the English vocabulary in the thirteenth century as a catchall term of abuse." Noting "such stock epithets as 'I hate thee as I do a Jew,' 'I would not have done so to a Jew,' and 'None but a Jew would have done so,'" he concludes that "the Jew as irredeemable alien and the Jew as bogeyman . . . coexisted at deep linguistic and psychological levels."[5] As John Gross puts the matter, "Nothing can alter the fact that, seen through the eyes of the other characters, Shylock is a deeply threatening figure, and that the threat he poses is of a peculiarly primitive kind."[6] We need to add that what "the eyes of the other characters" truly means, here, is "Elizabethan England," the citizens of which were of course the intended and the actual audience of the play (and the readers of its Quarto publication).

We also need to understand that Elizabethan England had only relatively recently been caught up in the Renaissance transformation of European economies. We know that, unlike Mediterranean economies, "there were no private moneychangers in medieval London" and that, although "from the fifteenth century onwards London goldsmiths were beginning to engage in deposit banking," no such effective system was in place in England until the end of the seventeenth century.[7] Thus, Europe's long record of hostility to money lending, and the interest charged thereon, had been largely dissipated in countries like Italy but lingered in countries like England. "By the end of the sixteenth century, . . . Jews were increasingly identified [in England] not with usury per se, but with outrageous and exploitative lending for profit."[8] Indeed, "Shakespeare's 'alien' Shylock cannot really be understood independent of the larger social tensions generated by aliens and their economic practices in London in the mid-1590s."[9] It is in no way surprising that "most moneylenders in Elizabethan literature were thoroughly sadistic."[10]

Accordingly, if we ask, as Martin D. Yaffe does, how "are we meant to understand Shylock's Jewishness," the answer seems reasonably clear.[11] Despite the power of Shylock's two speeches of protest, the nature of his Jewishness is both vague and elusive. Perhaps, for our purposes, today, it ought to be considered largely symbolic. Shakespeare's compatriots did not want or need more than that. It is therefore completely appropriate for that symbolic representation to say, as Shylock does at the approach of Antonio, "I hate him for he is a Christian" (1.3.36). It is equally appropriate for Shylock's daughter to say to Gobbo, the clown who is leaving Shylock's employ in order to be with a good Christian employer, "I am sorry thou wilt leave my father so. / Our house is hell, and thou a merry divel / Did'st rob it of some taste of tediousness" (2.3.1–3). Or for her to say, on the same subject, "But though I am a daughter to his [Shylock's] blood, / I am not to his manners" (2.3.7–8). Similarly, Lorenzo, Jessica's Christian lover and future husband, can declare with the absolute confidence of anyone who confronts a mere totem, "If e'er the Jew her father come to heaven, / It will be for his gentle daughter's sake" (2.4.34–35).

In short, "Shylock's stage-Judaism is a pseudo-religion, a fabrication: there is no true piety in it, and nothing to hold him back as he pursues his revenge."[12] We can no more go to *The Merchant of Venice* for perspectives on, or information about Jews and Judaism, than we can go *Hamlet* for guidance on Renaissance Danish manners and mores, or to *Anthony and Cleopatra* to help us understand Egypt during the great years of Rome. This is not to deprecate any of these splendid dramas, for no one in their right mind would or should approach Shakespeare's plays on non-English subjects in this way.

Still, *The Merchant of Venice* being a great play by the greatest of playwrights, the situation is inevitably somewhat more complex. Shakespeare's mind is so quick, his heart has so many deep and broad chambers, that he cannot simply sketch out his major figures as cartoon characters. He is as it were obliged to engage them as human beings. In the first of Shylock's two magnificently humanizing speeches, he speaks to Antonio, in the course of loan negotiations:

> Signior Antonio, many a time and oft
> In the Rialto you have rated me
> About my monies and my usances.
> Still have I borne it with a patient shrug
> (For sufferance is the badge of all our tribe).
> You call me misbeliever, cutthroat dog,
> And spit upon my Jewish gabardine,
> And all for use of that which is mine own.
> Well then, it now appears you need my help.
> Go to then, you come to me, and you say
> Shylock, we would have monies, you say so.
> You that did void your rheum upon my beard,
> And foot me as you spurn a stranger cur
> Over your threshold, monies is your suit.
> What should I say to you? Should I not say,
> Hath a dog money? Is it possible

A cur should lend three thousand ducats? Or
Shall I bend low, and in a bondman's key
With bated breath, and whispering humbleness,
Say this: Fair sir, you spat on me on Wednesday last,
You spurned me such a day, another time
You called me dog, and for these courtesies
I'll lend you thus much monies?

(1.3.100–122)

Shakespeare is not, in this speech, entering into any of the economic and religious issues that have been touched upon, albeit lightly, in this introductory essay. He is simply engaging, on levels few can reach, with a character in pain. He does this with Shylock on one more occasion, this time in prose rather than in verse:

I am a Jew. Hath not a Jew eyes? Hath not a Jew hands, organs, dimensions, senses, affections, passions, fed with the same food, hurt with the same weapons, subject to the same diseases, healed by the same means, warmed and cooled by the same winter and summer as a Christian is? If you prick us, do we not bleed? If you tickle us, do we not laugh? If you poison us, do we not die? And if you wrong us, shall we not revenge? If we are like you in the rest, we will resemble you in that. (3.1.49–57)

Shakespeare's intention in both these deservedly famous passages is not to justify Shylock's fierce cruelty. He is straightforwardly depicting a character, in the depth that he as a writer needed to attain. What he has achieved is in a sense a natural by-product of his genius rather than anything intrinsic to some general view of Jews and Jewishness, which is to some degree the nominal subject matter of his play. And Shylock's piercing humanity, as thus achieved, does not affect that nominal subject matter, any more than it does the narrative course of the play. Shylock is silenced and punished (both fiscally and by being compelled to accept baptism as a Christian) according to then-prevailing views of the fundamental nonhumanity of Jews and Jewishness. Is there a contradiction between the human Shylock and these attacks on what is obviously considered the nonhuman nature of Jews and Jewishness? Of course there is—if we attempt to frame *The Merchant of Venice* as an ideological drama, even an exposition of how Shakespeare himself viewed Jews and Jewishness. The play was no more conceived in such terms than *The Taming of the Shrew* was meant as a savage assault on women or than *The Tempest* was intended to be a close critique of magic or the behavior of magicians.

Recall the description of the play on the Quarto's 1600 title page. Antonio is clearly one of its three focal points, and he is a major player. But Shakespeare does little more with him than make him, as he makes Shylock, what the American novelist Henry James liked to call a *ficelle:* a stage device, used to pull plot strings. When he is required to be melancholy, he is melancholy, and when that need has passed, he ceases to be melancholy. When he is called upon to be somewhat unusually fond of Bassanio—though not so unusually fond as might appear in our twenty-first century, for there is absolutely nothing sexual in his part—Antonio ascends to the occasion. He can be loyal, he can be long-suffering—everything that he needs to be and, aside from the characteristic Shakespearean elegance with which he speaks, not a great deal more. Antonio works quite satisfactorily, in a role thus delimited; his characterization will not bear any large, close examination. For example, when he tells us, after the fact, why he thinks Shylock hates him, he claims circumstances never previously mentioned and not fully consistent with what has been told us: "He seeks my life, his reason well I know. / I oft delivered from his forfeitures / Many that have at times made moan to me, / Therefore he hates me" (3.3.21–24). The abusive episodes that Shylock has described are not here recalled. Neither is Antonio's bland statement, after Shylock's biting recitation, "I am as like to call thee so again, / To spit on thee again, to spurn thee too" (1.3.123–124). These are obviously not issues relevant to Antonio's *ficelle*-like status.

But the third and last-named of *Merchant*'s three centers of attention, Portia, has an immense part in the play's comedy of courtship and, finally, its light and witty romanticism—which occupies the whole of the fifth and last act. In act 1, scene 2, Portia is the very model of maidenly wisdom and, as to the other sex, cynicism. "I can easier teach twenty what were good to be done, than be one of the twenty to follow mine own teaching" (14–16). More directly, she asks her lady in waiting, Nerissa, "I may neither choose whom I would, nor refuse whom I dislike, so is the will of a living daughter curbed by the will of a dead father. Is it not hard, Nerissa, that I cannot choose one, nor refuse none?" (20–24). By the end of the scene, having rather scorchingly reviewed some of the many candidates for her hand, she sighs over yet another would-be husband: "If I could bid the fifth welcome with so good heart as I can bid the other four farewell, I should be glad of his approach. If he have the condition of a saint, and the complexion of a divel, I had rather he should shrive me than wive me. Come Nerissa. Sirrah go before. Whiles we shut the gate upon one wooer, another knocks at the door" (113–119).

She doggedly deals with, and is rid of, a number of failed suitors—until suddenly, there is an unknown and unnamed one announced by a messenger—that is, a servant. Portia's witty comments to the messenger, as she makes his break off his praise of this unknown, exhibit a new excitement: "No more, I pray thee. I am half afeared / Thou wilt say anon he is some kin to thee, / Thou spend'st such high-day wit in praising him" (2.9.96–98). The Elizabethan audience would have had no trouble understanding that the relative of a messenger would have no business courting a high-upper-class woman who consorts on equal terms with princes. This swift fillip, stirring up the courtship plot, is genially and very effectively tossed off.

In act 3, scene 2 we see Portia in a more sobered state. The unknown suitor has been the one she most wanted, Bassanio, and he is impatient to take the test that will either win her or lose her. "I would detain you here some month or two," she tells him, "Before you venture for me" (9–10). Plainly, she wants to be with him but not to risk being unable to be with him any longer, if he fails the test. She does not think he will fail it. But just the same, she is cautious. And he, male and impetuous (as well as fiscally desperate, a condition her immense wealth would instantly cure), wants to move ahead as quickly as possible. As he steps through the casket maze, sweet music is played, and sung, creating a perfect atmosphere for romantic success. Portia sees it coming, for she knows which choice would be the right one, and speaks in an aside of her maidenly wish not to hurry this wonderful thing to its death:

> O love, be moderate, allay thy ecstasy,
> In measure rein thy joy, scant this excess.
> I feel too much thy blessing, make it less,
> For fear I surfeit.
>
> (112–115)

He prevails—and makes the right choice, she is his. In a dazed, happy confusion he tells her he is "doubtful whether what I see be true, / Until confirmed, signed, ratified by you" (148–149). Portia speaks with a wisdom ripening right before our eyes:

> You see me, Lord Bassanio, where I stand,
> Such as I am. Though for myself alone
> I would not be ambitious in my wish
> To wish myself much better, yet for you
> I would be trebled twenty times myself,
> A thousand times more fair, ten thousand times
> More rich, that only to stand high in your account
> I might in virtues, beauties, livings, friends,
> Exceed account. But the full sum of me
> Is sum of something – which to term in gross,
> Is an unlessoned girl, unschooled, unpracticed,
> Happy in this, she is not yet so old
> But she may learn, happier than this,
> She is not bred so dull but she can learn.
>
> (150–163)

The glow of an exceedingly good marriage to come is all over her words. This is in the best sense comedy—that is, drama with a happy ending. Act 5 will extend this most beautifully.

But before Portia and Bassanio can reach that point, the danger Antonio is in, because of Shylock's fierce malice, must be dealt with. Bassanio rushes off to help. Portia, already wiser than he is in the real ways of the world, takes an indirect but distinctly more functional route. Knowing Antonio's is a case in law, being tried in court, she obtains from a learnèd cousin the best legal advice available—and also the appropriate legal robes, for she proposes to handle the case herself, in court. Armed and efficient, she sails into court, where the chief judge is the Duke of Venice himself.

| | |
|---|---|
| *Duke* | Came you from old Belario? |
| *Portia* | I did my lord. |
| *Duke* | You are welcome, take your place. |

    Are you acquainted with the difference

    That holds this present question in the court?

*Portia*    I am informed thoroughly of the cause.

    Which is the merchant here? And which the Jew?

(4.1.166–171)

Portia's disguise is complete and so effective that her husband (they have been married but their marriage has not yet been consummated) does not recognize her. Her masterly aplomb, indeed, is utterly lawyer-like. In fact, when she has ended the case in a completely satisfactory way (satisfactory, that is, to her side, which is of course the play's good side), she turns to the clerk of court and directs, "Clerk, draw a deed of gift" (4.1.391). It is a total triumph, and yet another blow in Shakespeare's continuing endeavor to prove that, all other things being equal, women tend to significantly overmatch the men they deal with.

Act 5 opens with one of the other two pairs of happy lovers, Lorenzo and Jessica (Shylock's daughter), sitting in the garden of Portia's magnificent house. It is night; the setting is replete with the stigmata of romance:

*Lorenzo*  The moon shines bright. In such a night as this,

    When the sweet wind did gently kiss the trees

    And they did make no noise, in such a night

    Troilus methinks mounted the Trojan walls,

And sighed his soul toward the Grecian tents
Where Cressed lay that night.

(5.1.1−6)

Lorenzo and his new-wedded wife, Jessica (escaped from a Jewish "hell" into a haven of Christianized happiness), prettily toss back and forth a deft mixture of blossoms and barbs. Lorenzo again romanticizes, once again to the sort of sweet music that earlier accompanied Bassanio's choosing among the three caskets:

How sweet the moonlight sleeps upon this bank.
Here will we sit, and let the sounds of music
Creep in our ears. Soft stillness, and the night,
Become the touches of sweet harmony.
Sit Jessica, look how the floor of heaven
Is thick inlayed with patens of bright gold.
There's not the smallest orb which thou beholdst
But in his motion like an angel sings,
Still choiring to the young-eyed cherubins.
Such harmony is in immortal souls,
But whilst this muddy vesture of decay
Doth grossly close in it, we cannot hear it

(53−64)

Portia and Nerissa (whose unconsummated marriage to Gratiano constitutes them the third wedding pair) arrive. Portia's first words strongly reinforce the tenor of act 5 thus far:

*Portia* That light we see is burning in my hall.
How far that little candle throws his beams.
So shines a good deed in a naughty world.

(88−90)

But Shakespeare is far too accomplished a dramatist to end the play simply with flowers and moonshine. There follows a lovely barrage of teasing banter, in the course of which both Portia and Nerissa show, yet again, how vastly their husbands are over-matched by them. The men are reduced to submissive admissions of guilt and pledges for a guilt-free future:

*Bassanio*                                         Nay, but hear me.
   Pardon this fault, and by my soul I swear
   I never more will break an oath with thee.

$$(246-248)$$

The play is thus all but finished. In a very few more lines, Portia leads them all indoors, for what is indicated will be a set of most acceptable tripartite acts of marital consummation.

## Notes

1. Spelling and punctuation modernized.
2. James Shapiro, *Shakespeare and the Jews* (New York: Columbia University Press, 1996), 76.
3. John Gross, *Shylock: A Legend and Its Legacy* (New York: Simon and Schuster, 1992), 18.
4. Shapiro, *Shakespeare and the Jews,* 134.
5. Shapiro, *Shakespeare and the Jews,* 24.
6. Gross, *Shylock,* 29.
7. Peter Spufford, *Power and Profit: The Merchant in Medieval Europe* (London: Thames and Hudson, 2002), 42.
8. Shapiro, *Shakespeare and the Jews,* 99.
9. Shapiro, *Shakespeare and the Jews,* 187.
10. Gross, *Shylock,* 50.
11. Martin D. Yaffe, *Shylock and the Jewish Question* (Baltimore: Johns Hopkins University Press, 1997), 4.
12. Gross, *Shylock,* 46.

# SOME ESSENTIALS OF THE SHAKESPEAREAN STAGE

## *The Stage*

- There was no *scenery* (backdrops, flats, and so on).

- Compared to today's elaborate, high-tech productions, the Elizabethan stage had few *on-stage* props. These were mostly handheld: a sword or dagger, a torch or candle, a cup or flask. Larger props, such as furniture, were used sparingly.

- Costumes (some of which were upper-class castoffs, belonging to the individual actors) were elaborate. As in most premodern and very hierarchical societies, clothing was the distinctive mark of who and what a person was.

- What the actors *spoke,* accordingly, contained both the dramatic and narrative material we have come to expect in a theater (or movie house) and (1) the setting, including details of the time of day, the weather, and so on, and (2) the occasion. The *dramaturgy* is thus very different from that of our own time, requiring much more attention to verbal and gestural matters. Strict realism was neither intended nor, under the circumstances, possible.

- There was *no curtain*. Actors entered and left via doors in the back of the stage, behind which was the "tiring-room," where actors put on or changed their costumes.

- In *public theaters* (which were open-air structures), there was no *lighting;* performances could take place only in daylight hours.

- For *private* theaters, located in large halls of aristocratic houses, candlelight illumination was possible.

### The Actors

- Actors worked in *professional,* for-profit companies, sometimes organized and owned by other actors, and sometimes by entrepreneurs who could afford to erect or rent the company's building. Public theaters could hold, on average, two thousand playgoers, most of whom viewed and listened while standing. Significant profits could be and were made. Private theaters were smaller, more exclusive.

- There was *no director.* A book-holder/prompter/props manager, standing in the tiring-room behind the backstage doors, worked from a text marked with entrances and exits and notations of any special effects required for that particular script. A few such books have survived. Actors had texts only of their own parts, speeches being cued to a few prior words. There were few and often no rehearsals, in our modern use of the term, though there was often some coaching of individuals. Since Shakespeare's England was largely an oral culture, actors learned their parts rapidly and retained them for years. This was *repertory* theater, repeating popular plays and introducing some new ones each season.

- *Women* were not permitted on the professional stage. Most female roles were acted by *boys;* elderly women were played by grown men.

## The Audience

- London's professional theater operated in what might be called a "red-light" district, featuring brothels, restaurants, and the kind of *open-air entertainment* then most popular, like bear-baiting (in which a bear, tied to a stake, was set on by dogs).

- A theater audience, like most of the population of Shakespeare's England, was largely made up of *illiterates.* Being able to read and write, however, had nothing to do with intelligence or concern with language, narrative, and characterization. People attracted to the theater tended to be both extremely verbal and extremely volatile. Actors were sometimes attacked, when the audience was dissatisfied; quarrels and fights were relatively common. Women were regularly in attendance, though no reliable statistics exist.

- Drama did not have the cultural esteem it has in our time, and plays were not regularly printed. Shakespeare's often appeared in book form, but not with any supervision or other involvement on his part. He wrote a good deal of nondramatic poetry as well, yet so far as we know he did not authorize or supervise *any* work of his that appeared in print during his lifetime.

- Playgoers, who had paid good money to see and hear, plainly gave dramatic performances careful, detailed attention. For some closer examination of such matters, see Burton Raffel, "Who Heard the Rhymes and How: Shakespeare's Dramaturgical Signals," *Oral Tradition* 11 (October 1996): 190–221, and Raffel, "Metrical Dramaturgy in Shakespeare's Earlier Plays," *CEA Critic* 57 (Spring–Summer 1995): 51–65.

# The Merchant of Venice

## CHARACTERS (DRAMATIS PERSONAE)

*The Duke of Venice*
*The Prince of Morocco* (Portia's suitor)
*The Prince of Arragon* (Portia's suitor)
*Antonio* (a merchant of Venice)
*Bassanio* (Antonio's friend, Portia's suitor)
*Solanio, Salarino, Gratiano* (friends of Antonio and Bassanio)
*Lorenzo* (in love with Jessica)
*Shylock* (a rich Jew)
*Tubal* (Shylock's friend)
*Lancelot Gobbo* (a clown, Shylock's servant)
*Old Gobbo* (Lancelot's father)
*Leonardo* (Bassanio's servant)
*Salerio* (Venetian court attendant)
*Balthasar, Stephano* (Portia's servants)
*Portia* (an heiress)
*Nerissa* (Portia's personal attendant)
*Jessica* (Shylock's daughter)
*Venetian Nobles, Officers of the Court of Justice, Jailer, Servants,* and
  *Attendants*

# Act I

### SCENE I

*Venice, a street*

ENTER ANTONIO, SALARINO, AND SOLANIO

*Antonio*  In sooth[1] I know not why I am so sad,
   It wearies me, you say it wearies you.
   But how I caught it, found it, or came by it,
   What stuff[2] 'tis made of, whereof it is borne,[3]
   I am to[4] learn. And such a want-wit[5] sadness makes of me,      5
   That I have much ado[6] to know myself.
*Salarino*  Your mind is tossing on the ocean,[7]
   There where your argosies[8] with portly[9] sail

---

1 truth
2 material
3 whereof it is borne=from where it has been carried
4 am to = still have to
5 witless/senseless/brainless person
6 labor, work
7 OHseeAHN
8 large merchant vessels★
9 stately, magnificent

Like signiors[10] and rich burghers[11] on the flood,[12]

10 Or as it were[13] the pageants[14] of the sea,

Do overpeer[15] the petty traffickers[16]

That curtsy[17] to them, do them reverence,[18]

As they[19] fly by them[20] with their woven wings.[21]

*Solanio* Believe me sir, had I such venture forth,[22]

15 The better[23] part of my affections[24] would

Be with my hopes[25] abroad. I should be still[26]

Plucking the grass[27] to know where sits[28] the wind,

Peering in maps[29] for ports, and piers, and roads.[30]

And every object[31] that might make me fear

20 Misfortune to my ventures, out of doubt[32]

10 the Signoria: hereditary noblemen who ruled Venice
11 i.e., northern European (Dutch or German) citizen-merchants
12 water
13 as it were = as one might say
14 decorated barges, festival street floats ("stage- or tapestry-scene")
15 look down on
16 petty traffickers = small/insignificant trader ships
17 deep bow, with one knee bent (then used for both men and women)
18 deference, respect
19 the argosies
20 the smaller ships
21 woven wings = winglike sails
22 venture forth = risky/hazardous business* under way
23 larger
24 emotions
25 wishes, expectations (i.e., the risks were great, but the profits would be much greater)
26 always
27 in order to toss it into the air (literally, to throw it to the winds)
28 where sits = from which direction blows
29 charts, maps
30 ports, and piers, and roads = harbors, and landing/unloading places, and sheltered places/roadsteads/anchorages near the shore
31 obstacle, hindrance
32 out of doubt = beyond a doubt ("certainly")*

Would make me sad.

*Salarino*               My wind[33] cooling my broth
Would blow me to an ague,[34] when[35] I thought
What harm a wind too great might do at sea.
I should not see the sandy hourglass[36] run
But I should think of shallows,[37] and of flats,[38]        25
And see my wealthy "Andrew"[39] docks[40] in sand,
Vailing[41] her high top lower than her ribs[42]
To kiss her burial.[43] Should I go to church
And see the holy edifice[44] of stone,
And not bethink me straight[45] of dangerous rocks,      30
Which touching but my gentle[46] vessel's side
Would scatter all her spices on the stream,[47]
Enrobe[48] the roaring waters with my silks,
And (in a word) but even now[49] worth this,
And now worth nothing. Shall I have the thought      35
To think on this, and shall I lack the thought

---

33 own breath
34 fever (EYgyoo)
35 when, if
36 sand-filled hourglasses were common; clocks were not
37 shallow-depth water
38 shoals (land just below the water's surface, and hard to see)
39 ship name
40 as she docks / is docked
41 lowering, bowing down
42 a ship's curved frame-timbers
43 kiss her burial = kiss / touch ("kiss the ground") her burial place / tomb
44 building
45 directly, at once★
46 noble★
47 water
48 dress, adorn
49 even now = recently, just now★

That such a thing bechanced[50] would make me sad?
But tell not me,[51] I know Antonio
Is sad to think upon[52] his merchandise.

40 *Antonio* Believe me no, I thank my fortune[53] for it,
My ventures are not in one bottom[54] trusted,
Nor to one place, nor is my whole estate[55]
Upon[56] the fortune of this present year.
Therefore my merchandise makes me not sad.

*Solanio* Why then you are in love.

45 *Antonio*                                                    Fie,[57] fie.

*Solanio* Not in love neither. Then let us say you are sad
Because you are not merry, and 'twere as easy
For you to laugh and leap, and say you are merry
Because you are not sad. Now by two-headed Janus,[58]

50 Nature hath framed[59] strange fellows in her time.
Some that will evermore peep[60] through their eyes,
And laugh like parrots at a bagpiper.[61]
And other[62] of such vinegar aspect,[63]

---

50 happening
51 tell not me = don't tell me
52 about, of
53 luck★
54 ship
55 condition, standing, fortune★
56 resting on
57 for shame!
58 Roman god of entrances and exits, beginnings and endings
59 shaped, constructed ("made")
60 look with narrowed/half-shut eyes
61 i.e., bagpipe music is wailingly sad, but parrots laugh at it
62 others (Elizabethan grammar was often more relaxed than we are, today, about issues of number, tense, and so on)
63 vinegar aspect = acid/sour face/look/appearance★

That they'll not show their teeth in[64] way of smile,

Though Nestor[65] swear the jest be laughable.                    55

ENTER BASSANIO, LORENZO, AND GRATIANO

*Solanio*   Here comes Bassanio, your most noble kinsman,

Gratiano, and Lorenzo. Fare ye well,

We leave you now with better company.[66]

*Salarino*   I would have stayed[67] till I had made you merry,

If worthier friends had not prevented[68] me.                    60

*Antonio*   Your worth is very dear[69] in my regard.

I take it your own business calls on you,

And you embrace th'occasion[70] to depart.

*Salarino*   Good morrow my good lords.

*Bassanio*   Good signiors both, when shall we laugh?[71] Say when?    65

You grow exceeding strange.[72] Must it be so?

*Salarino*   We'll make our leisures[73] to attend[74] on yours.

EXEUNT[75] SALARINO AND SOLANIO

*Lorenzo*   My Lord Bassanio, since you have found Antonio

We two will leave you, but at dinnertime

---

64 by
65 even Nestor, wise old Greek, notorious for his utter seriousness
66 companionship, society★
67 waited
68 (1) excelled, surpassed, (2) precluded, forestalled ("stopped")
69 precious, valuable
70 embrace th'occasion = accept/take advantage of the circumstances★
71 have a good time together
72 distant, foreign
73 free time, opportunities
74 accompany, wait upon, answer to, follow★
75 they exit (Latin plural of "exit")★

70    I pray[76] you have in mind where we must[77] meet.

*Bassanio*  I will not fail you.

*Gratiano*  You look not well signior Antonio,

You have too much respect upon[78] the world:[79]

They lose it[80] that do buy it with much care.[81]

75    Believe me you are marvelously[82] changed.

*Antonio*  I hold[83] the world but as the world Gratiano,

A stage, where every man must play a part,

And mine a sad one.

*Gratiano*           Let me[84] play the fool,

With mirth and laughter let old[85] wrinkles come,

80    And let my liver[86] rather heat with wine,

Than my heart cool with mortifying[87] groans.

Why should a man whose blood is warm within

Sit like his grandsire, cut in alabaster?[88]

Sleep when he wakes?[89] And creep[90] into the jaundice[91]

85    By being peevish?[92] I tell thee what Antonio,

---

76 ask, request
77 (1) are certain to, *or* (2) are supposed to
78 respect upon = concern for
79 (1) fortune, (2) worldly affairs
80 "the world"
81 trouble, anxiety, attention
82 astonishingly, surprisingly
83 view, think of, consider
84 let me = I would rather ("allow me")
85 old age's
86 regarded, then, as the location of high emotions, including courage★
87 (1) austere, self-denying, (2) deadly, fatal
88 i.e., a mortuary/funereal monument/statue
89 is awake
90 proceed cautiously/abjectly
91 deadly disease of the liver
92 morose, irritable

I love[93] thee, and it is my love that speaks.

There are a sort of men, whose visages

Do cream and mantle[94] like a standing[95] pond,

And do a willful stillness[96] entertain,

With purpose to be drest[97] in an opinion[98]                                90

Of wisdom, gravity,[99] profound conceit,[100]

As who should[101] say, I am sir an oracle,

And when I ope my lips, let no dog bark.

O my Antonio, I do know of these

That therefore only are reputed wise                                95

For saying[102] nothing, when I am very sure

If they should speak would almost damn those ears

Which, hearing them, would call their[103] brothers fools.

I'll tell thee more of this another time.

But fish not with this melancholy bait                                100

For this fool gudgeon,[104] this opinion.

Come good Lorenzo, fare ye well a while,

I'll end my exhortation[105] after dinner.

*Lorenzo*   Well, we will leave you then till dinnertime.

I must be one of these same dumb wise men,                                105

93 have genuine affection for★
94 cream and mantle = curdle and froth
95 stagnant
96 willful stillness = maintain/observe an obstinate/perverse refusal to speak
97 clothed
98 reputation
99 solemnity, authority
100 understanding, conception★
101 as who should = as if to
102 for saying = because they say
103 their own
104 small freshwater fish used as bait
105 earnest speech, urging moral behavior/thought

For Gratiano never lets me speak.

*Gratiano*  Well, keep me company but two years mo,[106]

Thou shalt not know the sound of thine own tongue.

*Antonio*  Fare you well, I'll grow a talker[107] for this gear.[108]

110 *Gratiano*  Thanks i'faith,[109] for silence is only commendable[110]

In a neat's[111] tongue dried,[112] and a maid[113] not vendible[114]

### EXEUNT GRATIANO AND LORENZO

*Antonio*  It is that anything, now.[115]

*Bassanio*  Gratiano speaks an infinite deal[116] of nothing, more

than any man in all Venice. His reasons[117] are two grains of

115 wheat hid in two bushels of chaff.[118] You shall[119] seek all day

ere[120] you find them, and when you have them they are not

worth the search.

*Antonio*  Well. Tell me now, what lady is the same

To whom you swore a secret pilgrimage[121]

120 That you today promised to tell me of?

*Bassanio*  'Tis not unknown to you Antonio

106 more, longer
107 grow a talker = become a conversationalist
108 for this gear = because of this (1) matter, (2) equipment ("these tools")
109 indeed*
110 proper, laudatory
111 ox, cow
112 i.e., a dried-up/withered old penis
113 virgin*
114 salable, marriageable
115 i.e., is what he just said anything at all?
116 amount, lot
117 views, arguments
118 husks left over after threshing
119 must
120 before*
121 sacred/holy journey

How much I have disabled mine estate,[122]
By something[123] showing a more swelling port[124]
Than my faint[125] means would grant continuance.[126]
Nor do I now make moan[127] to be abridged[128]          125
From such a noble rate,[129] but my chief care
Is to come fairly off[130] from the great debts
Wherein my time[131] something too prodigal[132]
Hath left me gaged.[133] To you Antonio
I owe the most in money and in love,          130
And from[134] your love I have a warranty[135]
To unburthen[136] all my plots[137] and purposes,
How to get clear of all the debts I owe.

*Antonio*   I pray you[138] good Bassanio let me know it,
And if it stand as you yourself still[139] do,          135
Within the eye[140] of honor, be assured

---

122  disabled mine estate = crippled/impaired my circumstances/fortune
123  to an extent
124  swelling port = inflated style of living
125  feeble
126  grant continuance = allow keeping on with
127  make moan = lament, complain
128  to be abridged = because I am reduced/curtailed
129  noble rate = great/magnificent quantity/size of expenditure
130  fairly off = (1) decently/properly, (2) fully away/out
131  wherein my time = in which my period/interval
132  something too prodigal = rather too extravagant*
133  pledged, mortgaged
134  because of
135  implied contract/guarantee (i.e., to Antonio, both as his warm friend and his largest creditor)
136  disclose
137  plans
138  I pray you = please
139  always? as yet? (the former more likely, but the latter not impossible)
140  recognition ("sight")

My purse, my person,[141] my extremest[142] means
Lie all unlocked[143] to your occasions.

*Bassanio*  In my schooldays, when I had lost one shaft[144]

140 I shot his fellow of[145] the selfsame flight
The selfsame way, with more advisèd watch,[146]
To find the other forth,[147] and by adventuring[148] both,
I oft found both. I urge this childhood proof[149]
Because what follows is pure innocence.

145 I owe you much, and like a willful youth
That which I owe[150] is lost, but if you please
To shoot another arrow that self[151] way
Which you did shoot the first, I do not doubt
As[152] I will watch the aim, or[153] to find both,

150 Or bring your latter hazard[154] back again,
And thankfully rest[155] debtor for the first.

*Antonio*  You know me well, and herein spend but[156] time
To wind[157] about my love with circumstance,[158]

141  my person = I myself ("my body")
142  uttermost
143  open
144  arrow
145  fellow of = another arrow on
146  advisèd watch = careful/deliberate/determined observation
147  also
148  risking
149  evidence, process, demonstration
150  (1) owe? *or* (2) own?
151  same
152  that
153  either
154  venture, chance, risk★
155  remain
156  spend but = you just spend
157  wriggle, circle
158  details, circumlocution

And out of doubt you do me now more wrong
In making question[159] of my uttermost[160]                           155
Than if you had made waste of all I have.
Then do but say to me what I should[161] do
That in your knowledge may by me be done,
And I am prest[162] unto it. Therefore speak.

*Bassanio*  In Belmont is a lady richly left,[163]                       160
And she is fair,[164] and fairer than that word,
Of wondrous virtues.[165] Sometimes from her eyes
I did receive fair speechless[166] messages.
Her name is Portia, nothing undervalued[167]
To Cato's daughter, Brutus' Portia.[168]                                165
Nor is the wide world ignorant of her worth,
For the four winds blow in from every coast
Renownèd[169] suitors, and her sunny locks
Hang on her temples like a golden fleece,
Which makes her seat of Belmont Cholchis' strond,[170]                  170
And many Jasons come in quest[171] of her.

---

159  making question = questioning, doubting
160  my uttermost = how far I am willing to go ("the very most")★
161  (1) must, (2) ought to
162  (1) thrust, urged, compelled, (2) enlisted
163  endowed by inheritance (i.e., as one "leaves" property by a will and
      testament)
164  beautiful★
165  qualities, conduct, moral excellence
166  wordless, silent
167  inferior
168  wife of Brutus, one of Caesar's assassins, and a woman of intense moral
      power
169  celebrated, honorable, of high reputation
170  makes her seat of Belmont Cholchis' strond = transforms her residence/
      country estate of Belmont into the shores of Colchis (where Jason had
      sought the Golden Fleece)
171  search, pursuit

O my Antonio, had I but the means
To hold a rival[172] place with one of them,
I have a mind presages[173] me such thrift[174]

175        That I should questionless[175] be fortunate.

*Antonio*  Thou knowst that all my fortunes are at sea,
Neither have I money, nor commodity[176]
To raise a present[177] sum. Therefore go[178] forth,
Try[179] what my credit can in Venice do,

180        That shall be racked[180] even to the uttermost
To furnish[181] thee to Belmont to[182] fair Portia.
Go presently inquire, and so will I,
Where money is, and I no question make[183]
To have it of my trust,[184] or for my sake.[185]

EXEUNT

172  competitive
173  a mind presages = a judgment/opinion that portends/predicts★
174  success, prosperity★
175  undoubtedly, without question
176  goods, property
177  immediate ("readily accessible")★
178  I will go
179  to see/test/find out★
180  stretched, strained
181  supply, provide for★
182  and to
183  no question make = have no doubt
184  of my trust = on my credit
185  for my sake = because of personal regard/considerations

## SCENE 2
### *Belmont, Portia's residence*

ENTER PORTIA WITH NERISSA, HER PERSONAL ATTENDANT

*Portia* By my troth[1] Nerissa, my little[2] body is aweary of this
great world.

*Nerissa* You would be sweet[3] madam, if your miseries were in
the same abundance as your good fortunes are. And yet for
ought I see, they[4] are as sick that surfeit[5] with too much, as 5
they that starve with nothing. It is no mean happiness
therefore to be seated[6] in the mean.[7] Superfluity[8] comes
sooner by white hair,[9] but competency[10] lives longer.

*Portia* Good sentences,[11] and well pronounced.[12]

*Nerissa* They would be better if well followed. 10

*Portia* If to do were as easy as to know what were good to do,
chapels[13] had been[14] churches, and poor men's cottages
princes' palaces. It is a good divine[15] that follows his own
instructions.[16] I can easier teach twenty what were good to

---

1 by my troth = in faith ("truly")
2 (1) short, (2) small
3 fine, feeling genial / agreeable
4 those
5 that surfeit = who feed to excess★
6 located, fixed
7 middle
8 excess, overabundance
9 comes sooner by white hair = brings white hair (aging) sooner
10 sufficiency, enough
11 opinions, wisdom ("sententia")
12 proclaimed, delivered
13 small private rooms for worship, not consecrated as churches
14 had been = would be
15 clergyman
16 teaching

15     be done, than be one of the twenty to follow mine own
teaching. The brain may devise[17] laws for the blood,[18]
but a hot temper leaps o'er a cold decree.[19] Such a hare is
madness,[20] the youth, to skip[21] o'er the meshes[22] of good
counsel,[23] the cripple.[24] But this reason[25] is not in fashion

20     to choose me a husband. O me, the word "choose." I may
neither choose whom I would, nor refuse whom I dislike, so
is the will[26] of a living daughter curbed[27] by the will[28] of a
dead father. Is it not hard,[29] Nerissa, that I cannot choose
one, nor refuse none?

25  *Nerissa*  Your father was ever[30] virtuous, and holy men at their
death have good inspirations.[31] Therefore the lottery[32] that
he hath devised in these three chests[33] of gold, silver, and
lead, whereof who chooses his meaning,[34] chooses[35] you,

17 contrive, arrange, invent, think out
18 emotions, passions
19 law, rule, order, judgment
20 folly
21 to skip = who leaps/hops
22 nets (i.e., as used to trap hares)
23 advice, direction
24 i.e., someone who cannot "skip"
25 logic, rationale, basis
26 wish, desire
27 controlled, restrained★
28 last will and testament
29 troublesome, fatiguing, difficult★
30 always★
31 good inspirations = exalted ideas
32 method of choosing/winning a prize by making a choice of other things
33 treasure chests/boxes (later referred to as "caskets")
34 whereof who chooses his meaning = from/by means of which whoever
chooses your father's meaning
35 i.e., will be enabled to marry

will no doubt ne'er[36] be chosen by any rightly but[37] one
who you shall rightly[38] love. But what warmth is there in          30
your affection towards any of these princely suitors that are
already come?

*Portia*  I pray thee overname[39] them, and as thou namest them,
I will describe them, and according to my description level
at[40] my affection.          35

*Nerissa*  First there is the Neapolitan prince.

*Portia*  Ay that's a colt[41] indeed, for he doth nothing but talk of
his horse, and he makes it a great appropriation[42] to his own
good parts[43] that he can shoe him[44] himself. I am much
afraid my lady his mother played false with a smith.[45]          40

*Nerissa*  Then is there the County Palantine.[46]

*Portia*  He doth nothing but frown, as who should say,[47] and[48]
you will not have me, choose.[49] He hears merry tales and
smiles not. I fear he will prove the weeping[50] philosopher
when he grows old, being so full of unmannerly[51] sadness in          45

36 never★
37 by any rightly but = correctly by anyone except
38 properly, truly, justly
39 name one after the other
40 level at = (1) focus on/take aim at, (2) balance out
41 awkward young person, young ass
42 special attribute
43 qualities, characteristics, talents★
44 the horse
45 played false with a smith = committed adultery with a blacksmith
46 County Palantine = royal count
47 as who should say = as if to say
48 if
49 choose someone else
50 melancholy (derived from misanthropic Heraclitus, Greek philosopher, ca. 540–480 B.C.E.)
51 rude, discourteous

his youth. I had rather to be married to a death's head[52] with
a bone in his mouth, then to either of these. God defend[53]
me from these two.

Nerissa How say you by[54] the French lord, Monsieur Le Bon?

50 Portia God made him,[55] and therefore let him pass for a man.
In truth I know it is a sin to be a mocker, but he, why he hath
a horse better than the Neapolitan's, a better bad habit of
frowning than the Count Palantine, he is every man in no
man.[56] If a throstle[57] sing, he falls straight a-capering,[58] he
55 will fence with his own shadow. If I should marry him, I
should marry twenty husbands. If he would despise[59] me, I
would forgive him,[60] for if he love me to[61] madness, I should
never requite[62] him.

Nerissa What say you then to Falconbridge, the young baron of
60 England?[63]

Portia You know I say nothing to him, for he understands not
me, nor I him. He hath[64] neither Latin, French, nor Italian,
and you will come into the court[65] and swear that I have a

---

52 death's head = skull (commonly used as a memento mori, a reminder of the
   inevitability of death)
53 protect
54 how say you by = what do you say/think of/about/concerning
55 i.e., he was born: God was understood to create everything
56 i.e., he tries to be everything/everyone, and succeeds in being nothing/no
   one
57 thrush
58 gay dancing/leaping
59 scorn, disregard ("go away")
60 forgive him = give him up
61 even to
62 return his love
63 baron of England = English baron
64 speaks/understands
65 court of law, in which one is sworn to tell the truth

poor pennyworth in the English.[66] He is a proper[67] man's
picture,[68] but alas, who can converse with a dumb show?[69]    65
How oddly he is suited.[70] I think he bought his doublet[71] in
Italy, his round hose[72] in France, his bonnet[73] in Germany,
and his behavior everywhere.

*Nerissa*    What think you of the Scottish lord, his neighbor?

*Portia*    That he hath a neighborly charity in him, for he    70
borrowed[74] a box of the ear of[75] the Englishman, and swore
he would pay him again when he was able. I think the
Frenchman became his surety,[76] and sealed[77] under[78] for
another.

*Nerissa*    How like you the young German, the Duke of Saxony's    75
nephew?

*Portia*    Very vilely[79] in the morning when he is sober, and most
vilely in the afternoon when he is drunk. When he is best, he
is a little worse than a man, and when he is worst, he is little

---

66 poor pennyworth in the English = a mere scrap of English
67 normal, real, actual
68 likeness
69 dumb show = theatrical representation★ without speech
70 dressed
71 jacketlike body garment, with or without sleeves
72 round hose = breeches-like garment, covering the legs, and padded to
   round it out
73 head, cap (all men wore hats/caps)
74 took, received
75 box of the ear of = blow on the head from
76 (1) guarantor, security, (2) protector, safeguard★
77 ratified (by signing and affixing a seal)★
78 i.e., a guarantor would sign underneath the signature of the primary debtor
   – perhaps meaning, here, that the Frenchman also received a blow on the
   head from the Englishman
79 awful, disgusting★

80     better than a beast. And the worst fall[80] that ever fell,[81] I hope
    I shall make shift[82] to go without him.

    *Nerissa* If he should offer to choose, and choose the right
    casket,[83] you should refuse to perform[84] your father's will, if
    you should refuse to accept him.

85     *Portia*   Therefore for fear of the worst, I pray thee set a deep[85]
    glass of Rhenish wine on the contrary[86] casket, for if the
    divel[87] be within,[88] and that temptation without,[89] I know
    he will choose it. I will do anything Nerissa, ere I will be
    married to a sponge.[90]

90     *Nerissa* You need not fear, lady, the having any of these lords.
    They have acquainted me with[91] their determinations,[92]
    which is indeed to return to their home and to trouble you
    with no more suit,[93] unless you may be won by some other
    sort[94] than your father's imposition,[95] depending on[96] the
95     caskets.

    *Portia*   If I live to be as old as Sibylla,[97] I will die as chaste as

---

80 (1) happening, occurrence,★ (2) calamity
81 happens
82 make shift = find a way
83 chest★
84 execute, carry out
85 full, large
86 wrong
87 devil
88 inside
89 outside
90 drunk (i.e., someone who soaks up alcohol)
91 acquainted me with = informed me of
92 decisions
93 pursuit, attendance, petitioning, supplication★
94 choice, luck, fortune
95 charge, order, command
96 depending on = contingent upon, conditioned by
97 the most famous Sibyl (oracle, prophetess), at Cumae, was said to have lived a
    thousand years

Diana,[98] unless I be obtained[99] by the manner of my father's
will. I am glad this parcel of wooers are so reasonable,[100] for
there is not one among them but I dote on[101] his very[102]
absence, and I wish them a fair departure.                          100

*Nerissa*  Do you not remember, lady, in your father's time, a
Venetian, a scholar and a soldier that came hither in company
of the Marquis of Mountferrat?

*Portia*   Yes, yes, it was Bassanio, as I think so was he called.

*Nerissa*  True madam, he of all the men that ever my foolish eyes   105
looked upon, was the best deserving[103] a fair lady.

*Portia*   I remember him well, and I remember him worthy of
thy praise.

ENTER A SERVANT

*Servant*  The four strangers seek you madam to take their leave.
And there is a fore-runner[104] come from a fifth, the Prince of   110
Morocco, who brings word the Prince his master will be here
tonight.

*Portia*   If I could bid the fifth welcome with so good heart
as I can bid the other four farewell, I should be glad of his
approach. If he have the condition[105] of a saint, and the         115
complexion[106] of a divel, I had rather he should shrive me[107]

98  moon goddess and protector of women
99  won★
100  rational, sensible
101  dote on = am infatuated with
102  true, actual, complete★
103  deserving of
104  herald
105  mode/state of being, moral nature
106  nature, character
107  shrive me = hear my confession (the precise meaning is uncertain)

than wive me. Come Nerissa. Sirrah[108] go before.[109] Whiles we shut the gate upon one wooer, another knocks at the door.

EXEUNT

108 term used in addressing males of low standing, or boys★
109 ahead of us

## SCENE 3
*Venice, a public place*

ENTER BASSANIO WITH SHYLOCK

*Shylock*   Three thousand ducats,[1] well.[2]

*Bassanio*   Ay sir, for three months.

*Shylock*   For three months, well.

*Bassanio*   For the which, as I told you, Antonio shall be bound.[3]

*Shylock*   Antonio shall become bound, well.                                      5

*Bassanio*   May you stead[4] me? Will you pleasure[5] me? Shall I
   know your answer?

*Shylock*   Three thousand ducats for three months, and Antonio
   bound.

*Bassanio*   Your answer to that?                                                 10

*Shylock*   Antonio is a good man.

*Bassanio*   Have you heard any imputation[6] to the contrary?

*Shylock*   Ho no, no, no, no. My meaning in saying he is a good
   man, is to have you understand me that he is sufficient,[7] yet
   his means are in supposition.[8] He hath an argosy bound to      15
   Tripolis,[9] another to the Indies, I understand moreover
   (upon[10] the Rialto)[11] he hath a third at Mexico, a fourth for

---

1 gold coins* (there was then no paper money)
2 fine? so?
3 contractually responsible
4 help, serve
5 gratify
6 accusation, charge
7 of adequate means/wealth
8 in supposition = uncertain, at risk
9 (1) in Lebanon, *or* (2) in Libya
10 from ("as heard upon")
11 Venetian mercantile exchange

England, and other ventures he hath squandered[12] abroad.
But ships are but boards, sailors but men, there be land rats,

20 and water rats, water thieves, and land thieves – I mean
pirates.[13] And then there is the peril of waters, winds, and
rocks. The man is notwithstanding[14] sufficient. Three
thousand ducats. I think I may take his bond.[15]

*Bassanio* Be assured you may.

25 *Shylock* I will be assured I may, and that[16] I may be assured,
I will bethink me.[17] May I speak with Antonio?

*Bassanio* If it please you to dine with us.

*Shylock* Yes, to smell pork, to eat of the habitation[18] which
your prophet the Nazarite[19] conjured the divel into.[20] I will

30 buy with you, sell with you, talk with you, walk with you, and
so following.[21] But I will not eat with you, drink with you,
nor pray with you. (*looking*) What news on the Rialto, who is
he comes here?

ENTER ANTONIO

*Bassanio* This is signior Antonio.

35 *Shylock* (*aside*) How like a fawning publican[22] he looks.

---

12 scattered
13 robbers
14 in spite of all that, nevertheless
15 contract/agreement of obligation/debt★
16 in order/how that
17 bethink me = consider
18 dwelling place (i.e., the place where pigs "dwell," the pigsty)
19 Jesus of Nazareth
20 Matt. 8:28–33
21 so following = so on, etc.
22 fawning publican = flattering/cringing inn-keeper ("publican" also means,
   biblically, "tax-gatherer," as in Luke 18:10; there is no reason to think
   Shylock so intends)

I hate him for[23] he is a Christian.
But more, for that in low simplicity[24]
He lends out money gratis,[25] and brings down
The rate of usance[26] here with us[27] in Venice.
If I can catch him once upon the hip,[28]                    40
I will feed fat[29] the ancient grudge[30] I bear him.
He hates our sacred nation,[31] and he rails[32]
Even there where merchants most do congregate
On me, my bargains,[33] and my well-won thrift,
Which he calls "interest." Cursèd be my tribe[34]           45
If I forgive him.

*Bassanio*                  Shylock, do you hear?

*Shylock*   I am debating of[35] my present store,
And by the near[36] guess of my memory
I cannot instantly raise up[37] the gross[38]
Of full three thousand ducats. What of that?                50

---

23 because
24 low simplicity = base ignorance
25 free of interest / charge
26 rate of usance = current interest rate (also then known as "usury")★
27 with us = (1) in Venetian moneylending? (2) in the Jewish community?
28 catch him ... upon the hip = get him ... at a disadvantage (a wrestling term)
29 fully, substantially, plentifully
30 ill-will (unless Shakespeare knew the long history of Christian persecution
   of Jews, which seems unlikely, this "ill-will" refers to communal hostility)
31 i.e., the Jews as God's chosen people (1Chron. 16:18)
32 speaks abusively
33 (1) bargaining, (2) contracts★
34 the Jewish people: the tribe of Israel
35 debating of = considering
36 closest
37 raise up = raise
38 whole

Tubal, a wealthy Hebrew of my tribe,[39]
Will furnish me. But soft,[40] how many months
Do you desire? (*to Antonio*) Rest you fair,[41] good signior,
Your worship[42] was the last man in our mouths.[43]

55 *Antonio* Shylock, albeit[44] I neither lend nor borrow
By taking nor by giving of excess,[45]
Yet to supply the ripe[46] wants of my friend
I'll break a custom. (*to Bassanio*) Is he yet possessed[47]
How much ye would?

*Shylock*                    Ay, three thousand ducats.

60 *Antonio* And for three months.

*Shylock* I had forgot, three months. (*to Bassanio*) You told me so.
(*to Antonio*) Well then, your bond. And let me see – but hear
you,
Methoughts[48] you said you neither lend nor borrow
Upon advantage.[49]

*Antonio*                    I do never use[50] it.

65 *Shylock* When Jacob grazed[51] his uncle Laban's sheep,[52]

---

39 (?) one of the twelve tribes of Israel (which makes no great sense; it seems an indication of how little Shakespeare knew about Jews)
40 not so fast★
41 rest you fair = be at ease
42 an honorific, in polite usage
43 in our mouths = of whom we spoke
44 although (allBEit)
45 extra, interest
46 urgent (i.e., that which is ripe must be harvested without delay; debts coming due must be paid; needs that have arisen must be met)
47 aware, have knowledge of
48 it seemed to me
49 upon advantage = for gain★ (interest)
50 do, engage in, practice★
51 tended, shepherded
52 (see Gen. 27)

This Jacob from our holy Abram[53] was
(As his wise mother wrought[54] in his behalf)
The third possessor.[55] Ay, he was the third.

*Antonio*  And what of him, did he take interest?

*Shylock*  No, not take interest, not as you would say          70
Directly[56] interest. Mark[57] what Jacob did,
When Laban and himself were compromised[58]
That all the eanlings[59] which were streaked and pied[60]
Should fall[61] as Jacob's hire.[62] The ewes being rank,[63]
In end of autumn turned to the rams,          75
And when the work of generation[64] was
Between these woolly breeders[65] in the act,[66]
The skillful shepherd pilled me[67] certain wands,[68]
And in the doing of the deed of kind[69]
He stuck them up before[70] the fulsome[71] ewes,          80
Who then conceiving, did in eaning time

53 Abraham
54 worked, arranged
55 i.e., (1) Abraham, (2) Isaac, (3) Jacob
56 straightforwardly, exactly
57 notice, observe★
58 were compromised = had agreed, come to terms, settled
59 young lambs
60 streaked and pied = striped and part-colored
61 be allotted/apportioned
62 wages, payment
63 in heat
64 procreation, propagation
65 propagators, procreators
66 in the act = being performed/done
67 pilled me = stripped, debarked (me: reflexive of no lexical significance)
68 sticks
69 deed of kind = act of procreation , the natural act ("sex")
70 in front of
71 (1) plump, fat, (2) lustful

Fall[72] parti–colored lambs,[73] and those were Jacob's.

This was a way to thrive,[74] and he was blest.

And thrift is blessing if men steal it not.

85 *Antonio* This was a venture sir, that Jacob served for,[75]

A thing not in his power to bring to pass,

But swayed and fashioned[76] by the hand of heaven.

Was this inserted[77] to make interest good?

Or is your gold and silver ewes and rams?

90 *Shylock* I cannot tell, I make it breed as fast,

But note me[78] signior.

*Antonio*                              Mark you this, Bassanio,

The divel can cite Scripture for his purpose.[79]

An evil soul producing holy witness[80]

Is like a villain with a smiling cheek,

95 A goodly[81] apple rotten at the heart.

O what a goodly outside falsehood hath.

*Shylock* Three thousand ducats, 'tis a good round sum.

Three months from twelve, then[82] let me see the rate.

*Antonio* Well Shylock, shall we be beholding[83] to you?

100 *Shylock* Signior Antonio, many a time and oft

---

72 drop, give birth to
73 i.e., whatever the mother (of any species) saw at the time of conception was thought to physically impress itself on her offspring
74 prosper, flourish, be successful★
75 served for = deserved, was worthy of, earned
76 swayed and fashioned = caused/ruled/governed★ and shaped
77 introduced, mentioned
78 note me = pay attention to me/what I say
79 the DIvel CAN cite SCRIPture FOR his PURpose
80 evidence, testimony, knowledge
81 good-looking
82 now
83 indebted, under obligation

In the Rialto you have rated[84] me
About my monies[85] and my usances.
Still[86] have I borne[87] it with a patient shrug
(For sufferance[88] is the badge[89] of all our tribe).
You call me misbeliever,[90] cutthroat[91] dog,                    105
And spit upon my Jewish gabardin,[92]
And all for use of that which is mine own.
Well then, it now appears you need my help.
Go to[93] then, you come to me, and you say
Shylock, we would[94] have monies, you say so.              110
You that did void[95] your rheum[96] upon my beard,
And foot[97] me as you spurn[98] a stranger cur[99]
Over[100] your threshold, monies is your suit.
What should I say to you? Should I not say,
Hath a dog money? Is it possible                                          115
A cur should lend three thousand ducats? Or

84  scolded, reproved
85  plural of "money" (most often used today in legal documents)
86  always, yet
87  endured
88  patient endurance, long-suffering
89  emblem, sign (Jews were often required to wear badges identifying them as
     Jews)
90  heretic, infidel
91  murderous
92  loose upper garment of coarse cloth
93  go to = come on
94  wish to
95  empty, discharge
96  mucous ("spit")
97  kick
98  kick at/away
99  worthless/low-bred dog
100  out across

Shall I bend low, and in a bondman's key[101]
With bated[102] breath, and whispering humbleness,
Say this: Fair sir, you spat on me on Wednesday last,
120 You spurned me such a day, another time
You called me dog, and for these courtesies
I'll lend you thus much monies?

  *Antonio*  I am as like to call thee so again,
To spit on thee again, to spurn thee too.
125 If thou wilt lend this money, lend it not
As to thy friends, for when did friendship take
A breed for barren metal[103] of[104] his friend?
But lend it rather to thine enemy,
Who if he break[105] thou mayst with better face
Exact[106] the penalty.

130 *Shylock*              Why look you how you storm,[107]
I would be friends with you, and have your love,
Forget the shames that you have stained[108] me with,
Supply your present wants, and take no doit[109]
Of usance for my monies, and you'll not hear[110] me,
135 This is kind[111] I offer.

---

101 bondman's key = serf's/slave's manner/voice/tone
102 lessened, subdued★
103 a breed for barren metal = a living thing in place of sterile (not living)
   metal (gold, silver, etc.)
104 from
105 (1) not fulfill his contractual obligation, (2) be fiscally ruined/bankrupted
106 demand, enforce★
107 rage, complain
108 i.e., to a significant degree literally stained
109 very small Dutch coin (DOYT)
110 listen to
111 (1) kindness, (2) a natural thing/process

*Bassanio*  This were[112] kindness.

*Shylock*                              This kindness will I show.

    Go with me to a notary,[113] seal me there

    Your single bond,[114] and in a merry sport[115]

    If you repay me not on such a day,

    In such a place, such sum or sums as are                    140

    Expressed[116] in the condition,[117] let the forfeit[118]

    Be nominated[119] for an equal[120] pound

    Of your fair flesh,[121] to be cut off and taken

    In what part of your body it pleaseth me.

*Antonio*  Content in faith, I'll seal to such a bond,                    145

    And say there is much kindness in the Jew.

*Bassanio*  You shall[122] not seal to such a bond for me,

    I'll rather dwell[123] in my necessity.

*Antonio*  Why fear not man, I will not forfeit it.

    Within these two months, that's a month before                    150

    This bond expires, I do expect return[124]

    Of thrice three times the value of this bond.

*Shylock*  O father Abram, what these Christians are,

112 would be
113 then more like a "solicitor" (non-court-appearing lawyer)
114 single bond = a contract without additional guarantors
115 jest, entertainment
116 set forth
117 stipulations, contractual terms
118 penalty for breach of contract
119 designated
120 exact, precise
121 Shapiro suggests that "flesh" here means "penis" (*Shakespeare and the Jews*, 121–122)
122 must
123 stay, remain
124 profits, cargoes

Whose own hard[125] dealings teaches them suspect[126]
155  The thoughts of others. Pray you tell me this,
If he should break his day, what should I gain
By the exaction of the forfeiture?
A pound of man's flesh taken from a man
Is not so estimable,[127] profitable neither[128]
160  As flesh of muttons, beefs, or goats.[129] I say
To buy his favor I extend this friendship.
If he will take it, so. If not adieu,
And for[130] my love I pray you wrong me not.

*Antonio*  Yes Shylock, I will seal unto this bond.

165 *Shylock*  Then meet me forthwith at the notary's,
Give[131] him direction[132] for this merry bond,
And[133] I will go and purse[134] the ducats straight,
See to my house (left in the fearful[135] guard
Of an unthrifty knave),[136] and presently
170  I'll be with you.

EXIT SHYLOCK

*Antonio*  Hie[137] thee, gentle Jew. This Hebrew will turn

125 callous, unfeeling
126 to be suspicious of
127 valuable
128 profitable neither = not as profitable as
129 muttons, beefs, or goats = sheep, cow, or goat carcasses
130 because of
131 to give
132 instructions
133 and then
134 collect
135 terrible, awful
136 unthrifty knave = wasteful/careless rascal★
137 hurry★

Christian, he grows kind.

*Bassanio* I like not fair terms, and a villain's mind.

*Antonio* Come on, in this there can be no dismay,[138]

My ships come home a month before the day.              175

EXEUNT

138  danger, difficulty

# Act 2

SCENE I

*Belmont, Portia's house*

TRUMPET FLOURISH[1]
ENTER MOROCCO, A TAWNY MOOR ALL IN WHITE,
AND THREE OR FOUR FOLLOWERS, WITH PORTIA, NERISSA,
AND THEIR TRAIN

*Morocco*  Mislike[2] me not for my complexion,[3]
The[4] shadowed livery[5] of the burnished[6] sun,
To whom I am a neighbor, and near bred.[7]
Bring me the fairest creature northward born,
5  Where Phoebus'[8] fire scarce thaws the icicles,
And let us make incision for[9] your love,
To prove whose blood is reddest, his or mine.

1 fanfare★
2 dislike
3 comPLEXeeOWN
4 which is the
5 shadowed livery = dark uniform
6 bright
7 near bred = closely related (i.e., to the sun as a god)
8 sun god
9 incision for = incisions/cuts through the skin on account of

I tell thee lady this aspect of mine
Hath feared[10] the valiant (by my love I swear).
The best regarded[11] virgins of our clime[12]                    10
Have loved it too. I would not change this hue,
Except to steal[13] your thoughts,[14] my gentle queen.

*Portia*    In terms of choice[15] I am not solely led
By nice direction[16] of a maiden's eyes.
Besides, the lottery of my destiny                               15
Bars[17] me the right of voluntary choosing.
But if my father had not scanted[18] me,
And hedged[19] me by his wit[20] to yield[21] myself
His[22] wife, who[23] wins me by that means I told you,
Yourself (renownèd prince) then stood as fair[24]               20
As any comer[25] I have looked on yet
For my affection.

*Morocco*                    Even for that I thank you.
Therefore I pray you lead me to the caskets
To try my fortune. By this scimitar[26]

10 frightened
11 respected, considered
12 climate, region
13 gain access to, take possession
14 attention, regard
15 in terms of choice = as far as choice is concerned
16 nice direction = the strict/particular/critical disposition/guidance
17 prevents
18 restricted, limited
19 bound, confined
20 ingenuity, wisdom★
21 yield myself = give myself as
22 as his
23 he who
24 stood as fair = had as good a chance, occupied as favorable a position
25 visitor, arrival
26 curved, single-edged sword

25   That slew the Sophy,[27] and a Persian Prince
     That won three fields of [28] Sultan Solyman,[29]
     I would oe'r-stare[30] the sternest[31] eyes that look,[32]
     Outbrave[33] the heart most[34] daring on the earth,
     Pluck[35] the young sucking cubs from the she-bear,
30   Yea, mock[36] the lion when he roars for prey,
     To[37] win thee, lady. But alas, the while
     If Hercules and Lichas[38] play at dice
     Which[39] is the better man, the greater throw
     May turn[40] by fortune from[41] the weaker hand.
35   So is Alcides[42] beaten by his rage,
     And so may I, blind fortune[43] leading me,
     Miss that[44] which one unworthier may attain,
     And die with[45] grieving.

*Portia*                         You must take your chance,

27 Shah of Persia
28 fields of = battles from
29 Turkish sultan, 1520–1566
30 outstare
31 harshest, grimmest
32 see
33 surpass, defy, outdo
34 which is most
35 snatch/drag/tear away
36 defy
37 in order to
38 Hercules' servant (LIEkas), thrown into the sea by his master after,
   unwittingly, Lichas brings him the poisoned shirt that kills him
39 to determine which
40 be spun/cast/thrown
41 by fortune from = by accident/luck away from
42 Greek name for Heracles (alSEEdeez)
43 i.e., luck, *not* the goddess Fortune, who was not portrayed as blind
44 miss that = fail to attain Portia
45 from/because of

And either not attempt to choose at all,

Or swear before you choose, if[46] you choose wrong          40

Never to speak to lady[47] afterward

In[48] way of marriage. Therefore be advised.[49]

*Morocco*  Nor will not.[50] Come, bring me unto my chance.

*Portia*    First forward[51] to the temple.[52] After dinner

Your hazard shall be made.

*Morocco*                          Good fortune then,          45

To make me blessed – or cursed'st among men.[53]

CORNETS[54]

EXEUNT

46 that if
47 any lady
48 by
49 warned, cautioned
50 nor will not = nor will I ever speak to another lady about marriage
51 first forward = first
52 church
53 to MAKE me BLESSED or CURsedst Among MEN
54 fanfare

## SCENE 2

*Venice, a street*

ENTER LANCELOT GOBBO

*Gobbo*  Certainly, my conscience will serve[1] me to run from[2]
this Jew my master. The fiend[3] is at mine elbow, and tempts
me, saying to me, "Gobbo, Lancelot Gobbo, good Lancelot,"
or "good Gobbo," or "good Lancelot Gobbo, use your legs,
5  take the start,[4] run away." My conscience says, "No, take heed
honest[5] Lancelot, take heed honest Gobbo," or as aforesaid
"honest Lancelot Gobbo, do not run, scorn running[6] with
thy heels." Well, the most courageous fiend bids[7] me pack.[8]
"Fia,"[9] says the fiend, "away," says the fiend, "for the heavens[10]
10  rouse[11] up a brave mind," says the fiend, "and run." Well, my
conscience hanging about the neck of my heart, says very
wisely to me, "My honest friend Lancelot, being an honest
man's son," or rather an honest woman's son, for indeed my
father did something smack,[12] something grow too,[13] he had
15  a kind of taste.[14] Well, my conscience says, "Lancelot budge[15]

1 (1) encourage, (2) permit
2 run from = abandon
3 Satan
4 i.e., get going
5 honorable, respectable, decent, proper★
6 such running
7 urges, orders, asks★
8 pack up, leave
9 get going ("via": VIEah)
10 for the heavens = for heaven's sake
11 raise, lift
12 savor (sexual)
13 i.e., his penis
14 a try, a savoring, etc. (sexual)
15 stir, move

not. "Budge," says the fiend." Budge not," says my conscience."
"Conscience," say I, "You counsel well," "Fiend," say I, "You
counsel well." To be ruled[16] by my conscience, I should stay
with the Jew my master, who (God bless the mark)[17] is a kind
of divel. And to run away from the Jew I should be ruled by          20
the fiend, who saving your reverence[18] is the divel himself.
Certainly the Jew is the very devil incarnation,[19] and in[20] my
conscience, my conscience is a kind of hard conscience, to
offer[21] to counsel me to stay with the Jew. The fiend gives the
more friendly counsel. I will run, fiend, my heels are at your     25
commandment, I will run.

ENTER OLD GOBBO WITH A BASKET

*Old Gobbo*  Master[22] young man, you I pray you, which is the
way[23] to Master Jew's?

*Gobbo*        (*aside*) O heavens, this is my true-begotten[24] father,
who being more than sand-blind[25] – high-gravel-blind[26] –        30
knows me not, I will try confusions with[27] him.

*Old Gobbo*  Master young gentleman, I pray you which is the
way to Master Jew's?

---

16 guided, governed, directed★
17 a more or less apologetic exclamation
18 saving your reverence = with all due respect (more or less apologetic)
19 incarnated ("made flesh")
20 to, in all
21 suggest, propose
22 mister
23 path, road★
24 i.e., "clown" English: Lancelot was truly begotten (engendered) *by* Old
   Gobbo, not vice versa
25 half-blind, dim-sighted
26 seriously stone-blind
27 confusions with = confusing

*Gobbo*      Turn upon your right hand[28] at the next turning,
35      but at the next turning of all on[29] your left. Marry,[30] at
the very next turning, turn of no hand,[31] but turn down
indirectly[32] to the Jew's house.

*Old Gobbo*  Be God's sonties,[33] 'twill be a hard way to hit.[34]
Can you tell me whether one Lancelot that dwells with him
40      dwell[35] with him or no?

*Gobbo*      Talk you of young Master Lancelot? (*aside*) Mark
me[36] now, now will I raise the waters.[37] (*to Old Gobbo*) Talk
you of young Master Lancelot?

*Old Gobbo*  No master sir, but a poor man's son, his father
45      (though I say't) is an honest, exceeding poor man, and God
be thanked well to live.[38]

*Gobbo*      Well, let his father be what 'a[39] will, we talk of
young Master Lancelot.

*Old Gobbo*  Your worship's[40] friend and[41] Lancelot, sir.

50  *Gobbo*      But I pray you ergo[42] old man, ergo I beseech you,
talk you of young Master Lancelot.

---

28 upon your right hand = to the right
29 to
30 a conventional exclamation (originally an evocation of Mary, mother of Christ)★
31 turn of no hand = don't turn at all
32 obliquely, slantwise, diagonally
33 be God's sonties = by God's saints (*santé,* in French)
34 reach
35 still lives
36 mark me = watch
37 old Gobbo's tears
38 well to live = prosperous, well-to-do
39 he
40 worship = honorific term of address for those of high standing
41 and his name is
42 therefore (Latin)

*Old Gobbo*  Of Lancelot, ant[43] please your mastership.

*Gobbo*      Ergo Master Lancelot, talk not of Master Lancelot,
father,[44] for the young gentleman according to fates and
destinies, and such odd[45] sayings, the sisters three,[46] and such      55
branches[47] of learning, is indeed[48] deceased, or as you would
say in plain terms,[49] gone to heaven.

*Old Gobbo*  Marry God forbid, the boy was the very staff of my
age, my very prop.[50]

*Gobbo*      Do I look like a cudgel[51] or a hovel-post,[52] a staff or      60
a prop? Do you know me, father?

*Old Gobbo*  Alack[53] the day, I know you not, young gentleman,
but I pray you tell me, is my boy – God rest his soul – alive or
dead?

*Gobbo*      Do you not know me, father?      65

*Old Gobbo*  Alack sir, I am sand-blind, I know you not.

*Gobbo*      Nay, indeed if you had your eyes you might[54] fail of
the knowing me. It is a wise father that knows his own child.
Well, old man, I will tell you news of your son, give me your
blessing, (*kneeling*) truth will come to light, murder cannot be      70
hid long, a man's son may,[55] but in the end truth will out.

43 and it, may it
44 old man
45 an indefinite number of
46 sisters three = the three Fates
47 divisions
48 in fact
49 words*
50 support (as in "support beam")
51 short, thick stick ("club")
52 shed-post
53 alas
54 might still
55 be hidden

*Old Gobbo* Pray you sir stand up, I am sure you are not Lancelot my boy.

*Gobbo* Pray you let's have no more fooling about it, but give
75 me your blessing. I am Lancelot your boy that was, your son that is, your child that shall be.

*Old Gobbo* I cannot think you are my son.

*Gobbo* I know not what I shall[56] think of that. But I am Lancelot the Jew's man, and I am sure Margery your wife is
80 my mother.

*Old Gobbo* Her name is Margery indeed, I'll be sworn if thou be Lancelot, thou art mine own flesh and blood. Lord worshipped might he be! (*touching the back of Gobbo's head*) What a beard hast thou got, thou hast got more hair on thy
85 chin than Dobbin my fill-horse[57] has on his tail.

*Gobbo* It should[58] seem then that Dobbin's tail grows backward. I am sure he had more hair of[59] his tail than I have[60] of my face when I last saw him.

*Old Gobbo* Lord how art thou changed. How dost thou and thy
90 master agree?[61] I have brought him a present. How 'gree you now?

*Gobbo* Well, well, but for mine own part, as I have set up my rest[62] to run away, so I will not rest till I have run some[63]

56 ought to, must
57 shaft-horse (i.e., the rear horse in a team, the one put into the shafts/long bars attached to the harness and to the wagon)
58 would, must
59 on
60 had
61 get along
62 set up my rest = determined to venture my last stake/reserve (as in gambling)
63 a certain (indefinite) amount of

ground. My master's a very Jew, give him a present, give him a
halter,[64] I am famished in his service. You may tell[65] every       95
finger I have with my ribs.[66] Father, I am glad you are come,
give me[67] your present to one Master Bassanio, who indeed
gives rare new liveries.[68] If I serve not him, I will run as far as
God has any ground.[69] O rare fortune, here comes the man.
To[70] him father, for I am a Jew if I serve the Jew any longer.       100

ENTER BASSANIO WITH AN ATTENDANT OR TWO

*Bassanio*     (*to Attendants*) You may do so, but let it be so hasted[71]
that supper be ready at the farthest by five of the clock. See
these letters delivered, put the liveries to making, and desire
Gratiano to come anon[72] to my lodging.

*Gobbo*        To him father.                                          105

*Old Gobbo*  God bless your worship.

*Bassanio*     Gramercy.[73] Would'st[74] thou aught[75] with me?

*Old Gobbo*  Here's my son sir, a poor boy –

*Gobbo*        Not a poor boy sir, but the rich Jew's man that
would, sir, as my father shall specify.[76]                           110

---

64 hangman's noose
65 recognize, perceive, distinguish
66 clown language for "every rib I have with your fingers"
67 give me = give on my behalf/for me
68 rare new liveries = exceptional/fine new servants' uniforms★
69 i.e., as far as the world goes/extends
70 go to/at
71 so hasted = done so quickly
72 at once★
73 thank you
74 do you wish/want
75 anything, something
76 speak of in detail

*Old Gobbo*  He hath a great infection[77] sir, as one would say, to serve –

*Gobbo*  Indeed the short and the long is, I serve the Jew, and have a desire as my father shall specify.

115  *Old Gobbo*  His master and he (saving your worship's reverence) are scarce cater-cousins[78] –

*Gobbo*  To be brief, the very truth is that the Jew, having done me wrong, doth cause me, as my father being I hope an old man shall frutify[79] unto you –

120  *Old Gobbo*  I have here a dish of doves[80] that I would bestow upon[81] your worship, and my suit is –

*Gobbo*  In very brief, the suit is impertinent[82] to myself, as your worship shall know by this honest old man, and though I say it, though old man, yet poor man, my father.

125  *Bassanio*  One[83] speak for both. What would you?

*Gobbo*  Serve you sir.

*Old Gobbo*  That is the very defect[84] of the matter sir.

*Bassanio*  I know thee well, thou hast obtained thy suit.
Shylock thy master spoke with me this day,

130  And hath preferred[85] thee (if it be preferment[86]
To leave a rich Jew's service) to become

---

77 affection ("desire") (uneducated man's error)
78 good/intimate friends
79 notify (uneducated man's error)
80 of doves = made of/from doves/pigeons
81 bestow upon = give/present* to
82 pertinent ("relevant") (uneducated man's error)
83 let one of you
84 effect ("purpose, intent") (uneducated man's error)
85 recommended
86 a promotion

The follower of so poor a gentleman.[87]

Gobbo    The old proverb[88] is very well parted[89] between my
master Shylock and you sir. You have the "grace of God," sir,
and he hath "enough."    135

Bassanio    Thou speakst it well. (*to Old Gobbo*) Go, father, with
thy son.

(*to Gobbo*) Take leave of thy old[90] master, and inquire
My lodging out. (*to Attendants*) Give him a livery
More guarded[91] than his fellows'. See it done.

Gobbo    Father, in. I cannot get a service,[92] no, I have ne'er a    140
tongue in my head.[93] Well. (*pretending to read his own palm*) If
any man in Italy have a fairer table[94] which doth offer[95] to
swear upon a book![96] I shall have good fortune. Go to, here's
a simple[97] line of life,[98] here's a small trifle[99] of wives. Alas,
fifteen wives is nothing, eleven widows and nine maids is a    145
simple coming in[100] for one man. And then to 'scape
drowning thrice, and to be in peril of my life with[101] the
edge of a featherbed.[102] Here are simple 'scapes. Well, if

87  i.e., so poor a gentleman as myself
88  "the grace of God is gear [property] enough"
89  divided
90  former
91  ornamented
92  job as a domestic servant
93  (?) quoting from his father's strictures, when Gobbo was younger
94  palm
95  present itself
96  i.e., oaths were (and still are) taken with one hand on the Bible
97  straightforward
98  line of life = life-determining line in the palm
99  insignificant total
100  simple coming in = humble beginning
101  from
102  soft bed, stuffed with feathers (or down) (edge = the sharp/cutting edge of

Fortune[103] be a woman, she's a good wench[104] for this
150  gear.[105] Father come, I'll take my leave of the Jew in the[106]
twinkling.

EXIT GOBBO AND OLD GOBBO

*Bassanio*  I pray thee, good Leonardo, think on[107] this.
These things being bought and orderly bestowed,[108]
Return in haste, for I do feast[109] tonight
155  My best esteemed[110] acquaintance. Hie thee, go.
*Leonardo*  My best endeavors[111] shall be done herein.[112]

ENTER GRATIANO

*Gratiano*  Where's your master?
*Leonardo*                                 Yonder sir, he walks.

EXIT LEONARDO

*Gratiano*  Signior Bassanio.
*Bassanio*  Gratiano.
*Gratiano*  I have a suit to you.
160  *Bassanio*                                 You have obtained it.

---

a blade: the sense seems to be that getting into bed with a woman –
marrying her – is as dangerous as being attacked with a knife)
103  the goddess*
104  lively young woman
105  (?) clothing, dress
106  a
107  think on = apply yourself to
108  orderly bestowed = properly (1) used, (2) placed
109  (verb) entertain sumptuously
110  valued, respected
111  efforts
112  in this matter

*Gratiano*  You must not deny[113] me, I must go with you to
  Belmont.
*Bassanio*  Why then you must. But hear thee Gratiano,
  Thou art too wild,[114] too rude,[115] and bold[116] of voice,
  Parts that become[117] thee happily[118] enough,
  And in such eyes as ours appear not faults,                    165
  But where they are not known, why there they show[119]
  Something too liberal.[120] Pray thee take pain[121]
  To allay[122] with some cold drops of modesty[123]
  Thy skipping[124] spirit, lest through thy wild behavior
  I be misconstered[125] in the place I go to,                   170
  And lose my hopes.
*Gratiano*                 Signor Bassanio, hear me.
  If I do not put on a sober habit,[126]
  Talk with respect, and swear but[127] now and then,
  Wear[128] prayerbooks in my pocket, look demurely,[129]

113  refuse, say no to★
114  uncultured, unrestrained
115  unskilled, barbarous
116  presumptuous
117  suit, are fitting for★
118  successfully, satisfactorily, aptly
119  look, are viewed as
120  something too liberal = somewhat/rather too free/unrestrained★
121  take pain = make an effort★
122  repress, calm
123  self-control, moderation
124  leaping, jumping
125  misconstrued (missCONstered)
126  sober habit = moderate/solemn/serious/sedate★ behavior *and/or*
     clothing★
127  only
128  carry
129  modestly, gravely, quietly

175     Nay more, while grace is saying,[130] hood[131] mine eyes

       Thus with my hat, and sigh and say "amen,"

       Use all the observance of civility[132]

       Like one well studied in a sad ostent[133]

       To please his grandam, never trust me more.

180  *Bassanio*  Well, we shall see your bearing.[134]

    *Gratiano*  Nay, but I bar[135] tonight, you shall not gage[136] me

      By what we do tonight.

    *Bassanio*                No, that were pity.[137]

      I would entreat you rather to put on

      Your boldest suit[138] of mirth, for we have friends

185      That purpose[139] merriment. But fare you well,

      I have some business.

    *Gratiano*  And I must to Lorenzo and the rest.

      But we will visit you at supper time.

EXEUNT

130  being said
131  cover (with his hat's brim)
132  good behavior ("citizenship")
133  showing, display (Latin *ostentatio*)★
134  behavior
135  but I bar = unless I (1) stop myself, (2) behave myself (a pun: "bear" and "bar" were quasi-homophonic)
136  shall not gage = must not judge
137  that were pity = that would be a pity
138  (1) clothing, (2), condition, state (i.e., Bassanio answers Gratiano's pun with a pun of his own)
139  intend

## SCENE 3

*Shylock's house*

ENTER JESSICA AND GOBBO

*Jessica*  I am sorry thou wilt leave my father so.
 Our house is hell, and thou a merry divel
 Did'st rob it of some taste[1] of tediousness.[2]
 But fare thee well, there is a ducat for thee.
 And Lancelot, soon at supper shalt thou see      5
 Lorenzo, who is thy new master's guest.
 Give him this letter, do it secretly.
 And so farewell: I would not have my father
 See me in talk with thee.

*Gobbo*  Adieu, tears exhibit[3] my tongue. Most beautiful pagan,   10
 most sweet Jew, if a Christian do not play the knave and get
 thee, I am much deceived. But adieu, these foolish drops do
 somewhat drown my manly spirit. Adieu.

EXIT GOBBO

*Jessica*  Farewell good Lancelot.
 Alack, what heinous[4] sin is it in me        15
 To be ashamed to be my father's child?
 But though I am a daughter to his blood,
 I am not[5] to his manners.[6] O Lorenzo,
 If thou keep promise I shall end this strife,
 Become a Christian, and thy loving wife.      20

EXIT

1 sense, flavor
2 weariness, exhaustion, boredom★
3 inhibit (uneducated man's error)
4 atrocious, infamous, hateful (HAYnes)
5 not a daughter
6 way of life, behavior, morals

49

## SCENE 4

*Venice, a street*

ENTER GRATIANO, LORENZO, SALARINO, AND SOLANIO

*Lorenzo*   Nay, we will slink[1] away in supper time,
   Disguise us at my lodging, and return
   All in an hour.

*Gratiano*   We have not made good preparation.[2]

5   *Salarino*   We have not spoke[3] us yet of torchbearers.

*Solanio*   'Tis vile unless it may be quaintly[4] ordered,
   And better in my mind not undertook.

*Lorenzo*   'Tis now but four of clock, we have two hours
   To furnish us.

ENTER GOBBO WITH LETTER

         Friend Lancelot. What's the news?

10   *Gobbo*   And it shall please you to break up[5] this, shall it[6] seem
   to signify.[7]

*Lorenzo*   I know the hand,[8] in faith 'tis a fair hand,
   And whiter than the paper it writ on
   Is the fair hand that writ.

*Gratiano*                         Love news, in faith.

15   *Gobbo*   By your leave sir.[9]

---

1 slip, steal
2 PREperAseeOWN
3 (1) spoken, discussed, (2) requested, engaged
4 cleverly, skillfully
5 break up = break the seal on ("open")
6 shall it = it shall/will
7 i.e., inform you of the news
8 handwriting
9 by your leave sir = with your permission★ sir (I will leave)

*Lorenzo*   Whither goest thou?

*Gobbo*   Marry sir, to bid[10] my old master the Jew to sup
tonight with my new master the Christian.

*Lorenzo*   Hold here, take this. (*gives money*) Tell gentle Jessica
I will not fail her, speak it privately.                           20
Go gentlemen,
Will you prepare you for this masque[11] tonight?
I am provided of[12] a torchbearer.

EXIT GOBBO

*Salarino*   Ay marry, I'll be gone about it straight.

*Solanio*   And so will I.                                          25

*Lorenzo*   Meet me and Gratiano at Gratiano's lodging
Some[13] hour hence.

*Salarino*   'Tis good we do so.

EXEUNT SALARINO AND SOLANIO

*Gratiano*   Was not that letter from fair Jessica?

*Lorenzo*   I must needs tell thee all. She hath directed[14]         30
How I shall[15] take her from her father's house,
What gold and jewels she is furnished with,
What page's suit[16] she hath in readiness.
If e'er[17] the Jew her father come to heaven,

10 invite
11 entertainment (music, dancing, and miming) in which the performers wear
   masks
12 am provided of = have obtained
13 about an
14 written
15 must
16 page's suit = boy/youth's clothing
17 ever

35   It will be for his gentle daughter's sake.
     And never dare misfortune cross her foot,[18]
     Unless she[19] do it under this excuse,
     That she[20] is issue[21] to a faithless[22] Jew.
     Come go with me, peruse this[23] as thou goest.
40   Fair Jessica shall be my torchbearer.

EXEUNT

18 path ("where her foot walks")
19 it (Fortune, a goddess, is feminine; misfortune, though not a goddess, thereby
    acquires feminine gender)
20 Jessica
21 child
22 (1) unbelieving (in Christianity), (2) treacherous, untrustworthy
23 peruse this = examine/read her letter

## SCENE 5

*Venice, in front of Shylock's house*

ENTER SHYLOCK AND GOBBO

*Shylock*  Well, thou shall see (thy eyes shall be thy judge)

The difference of¹ old Shylock and Bassanio.

(*calling*) What Jessica! (*to Gobbo*) Thou shalt not gormandize²

As thou hast done with me. What Jessica?

And³ sleep, and snore, and rend⁴ apparel out.                    5

Why Jessica, I say!

*Gobbo*  Why Jessica!

*Shylock*  Who bids thee call? I do not bid thee call.

*Gobbo*  Your worship was wont⁵ to tell me I could do nothing

without bidding.⁶                                                10

ENTER JESSICA

*Jessica*  Call you? What is your will?⁷

*Shylock*  I am bid forth to supper, Jessica,

There are my keys. But wherefore⁸ should I go?

I am not bid for love, they flatter me.

But yet I'll go in hate, to feed upon⁹                           15

The prodigal¹⁰ Christian. Jessica my girl,

1 between
2 eat like a glutton
3 and all you ever do is
4 wear out ("tear apart")
5 accustomed
6 i.e., I couldn't/wouldn't do anything unless I was told to do it
7 what is your will = what is it you wish/want
8 why
9 by means/at the expense of
10 extravagant, wasteful

Look to[11] my house. I am right loath to go,
There is some ill a-brewing[12] towards my rest,[13]
For I did dream of money bags tonight.[14]

20   *Gobbo*   I beseech you sir, go, my young master doth expect your
         reproach.[15]

*Shylock*   So do I his.

*Gobbo*   And they have conspired[16] together. I will not say you
         shall see a masque, but if you do, then it was not for nothing

25       that my nose fell a-bleeding on Black Monday[17] last, at six
         o'clock i' the morning, falling out[18] that year on Ash
         Wednesday was four year in th' afternoon.[19]

*Shylock*   What, are there masques? Hear you me, Jessica,
         Lock up my doors, and when you hear the drum

30       And the vile squealing of the wry-necked fife,[20]
         Clamber[21] not you up to the casements[22] then,
         Nor thrust your head into the public street
         To gaze on Christian fools with varnished[23] faces.
         But stop[24] my house's ears, I mean my casements,

11 look to = attend to, take care of ★
12 in preparation
13 peace, tranquillity
14 last night
15 approach (reproach = disgrace / shame / censure) (uneducated man's error)
16 cooperated, planned
17 Black Monday = Easter Monday
18 falling out = coming on
19 Gobbo, a clown figure, is (1) making fun of astrological and other
   predictions, and (2) making no great sense
20 wry-necked fife = bent / contorted neck of the flute player (facing at a right
   angle to his instrument)
21 climb
22 window frames
23 painted ★
24 close up, plug

54

Let not the sound of shallow foppery[25] enter                          35
My sober house. By Jacob's staff[26] I swear,
I have no mind[27] of feasting forth[28] tonight.
But I will go. Go you before me sirrah,
Say I will come.

*Gobbo*  I will go before sir.                                          40
(*aside to Jessica*) Mistress, look out at window for all this.
There will come a Christian by,[29]
Will be worth a Jewès[30] eye.

*Shylock*  What says that fool of Hagar's[31] offspring, ha?

*Jessica*  His words were "farewell mistress," nothing else.          45

*Shylock*  The patch[32] is kind enough, but a huge feeder,
Snail-slow in profit,[33] and he sleeps by day
More than the wildcat.[34] Drones hive not[35] with me,
Therefore I part with him, and part with him
To one that I would have him help to waste                              50
His borrowed purse.[36] Well, Jessica go in,
Perhaps I will return immediately.
Do as I bid you, shut doors after you.

25 shallow foppery = superficial folly / affectation
26 "With my staff I passed over this Jordan; and now I am become two bands
    [companies, troops]" (Gen. 32:10)
27 desire, wish
28 away from home
29 nearby*
30 the spelling is from the Quarto; the accent mark is an editorial addition, to
    make clear that the word is meant to be pronounced with two syllables
31 Abraham's cast-out servant, mother of Ishmael (Gen. 21:9–21)
32 fool, clown, booby
33 benefit, gain
34 hunting at night, and sleeping all day
35 drones hive not = nonworkers (like drone bees) don't take shelter
36 funds

Fast bind,[37] fast find,[38]

55 A proverb never stale in thrifty mind.

EXIT SHYLOCK

*Jessica* Farewell, and if my fortune be not crossed,[39]
  I have a father, you a daughter lost.

EXIT JESSICA

37 tie things up securely / tightly
38 surely find them when you want them
39 fortune be not crossed = luck is not blocked / thwarted

## SCENE 6

*Venice, in front of Shylock's house*

ENTER GRATIANO AND SALARINO, AS MASQUERS

*Gratiano*  This is the penthouse[1] under which Lorenzo
  Desired us to make stand.[2]

*Salarino*                                  His hour[3] is almost past.

*Gratiano*  And it is mervail[4] he outdwells[5] his hour,
  For lovers ever run before[6] the clock.

*Salarino*   O ten times faster Venus' pigeons[7] fly                         5
  To seal[8] love's bonds new-made, than they are wont
  To keep obligèd faith unforfeited.[9]

*Gratiano*  That ever holds.[10]  Who riseth from a feast
  With that keen appetite that he sits down?
  Where is the horse that doth untread[11] again                             10
  His tedious measures[12] with the unbated[13] fire
  That he did pace them first? All things that are,
  Are with more spirit chased[14] than enjoyed.

1 porch, gallery
2 a pause/delay
3 appointed time
4 wonderful, marvelous
5 tarries beyond
6 ahead of
7 doves, who draw Venus' chariot
8 ratify, authenticate
9 keep obligèd faith unforfeited = preserve from violation faith that has
  already been pledged
10 applies, is unbroken/observed
11 retrace
12 paces ("distance")s
13 unabated, unblunted
14 spirit chased = liveliness pursued/hunted

How like a younger[15] or a prodigal
15    The scarfèd bark[16] puts from her native bay,[17]
Hugged and embracèd by the strumpet[18] wind![19]
How like a prodigal doth she return
With overweathered ribs and ragged sails,
Lean, rent, and beggared[20] by the strumpet wind?[21]

ENTER LORENZO

20  *Salarino*  Here comes Lorenzo, more of this hereafter.
    *Lorenzo*  Sweet friends, your patience for my long abode.[22]
Not I, but my affairs have made you wait.
When you shall please to play the thieves for wives,
I'll watch as long for you then. Approach.
25    Here dwells my father[23] Jew. Hoa, who's within?

JESSICA ABOVE[24]

    *Jessica*    Who are you? Tell me for more certainty,
Albeit[25] I'll swear that I do know your tongue.[26]
    *Lorenzo*  Lorenzo, and thy love.
    *Jessica*    Lorenzo certain, and my love indeed,[27]
30    For who love I so much? And now who knows

---

15 younger son
16 scarfèd bark = banner-decorated ship
17 i.e., harbor
18 whorelike
19 then pronounced to rhyme with "bind, mind, find"
20 made destitute
21 lean RENT and BEGgared BY the STRUMpet WIND
22 delay
23 marriage (pledged or accomplished) turned in-laws into family members
24 on a theatrical "balcony"
25 although ("all be it")
26 voice
27 truly

But you Lorenzo, whether I am yours?

*Lorenzo*  Heaven and thy thoughts are witness that thou art.

*Jessica*    Here, catch this casket, it is worth the pains.

I am glad 'tis night, you[28] do not look on me,

For I am much ashamed of my exchange.[29]                35

But love is blind, and lovers cannot see

The pretty[30] follies that themselves commit,

For if they could, Cupid[31] himself would blush

To see me thus transformèd to a boy.

*Lorenzo*  Descend, for you must be my torchbearer.          40

*Jessica*    What, must I hold a candle to my shames?

They in themselves (goodsooth) are too too light.[32]

Why, 'tis an office[33] of discovery, love,

And I should be obscured.[34]

*Lorenzo*                                    So are you sweet,

Even in the lovely garnish[35] of a boy.                       45

But come at once,

For the close[36] night doth play the runaway,[37]

And we are stayed for at Bassanio's feast.

*Jessica*    I will make fast the doors and gild[38] myself

With some more ducats, and be with you straight.          50

EXIT JESSICA

28 and you
29 transmutation, alteration, substitution
30 fine (negative sense)
31 who was often pictured as blind
32 (1) bright, luminous, (2) frivolous
33 function, employment★
34 should be obscured = ought to be hidden
35 outfit, clothing
36 private, secluded, secret
37 deserter (i.e., it is rapidly leaving us)
38 make golden

*Gratiano*  Now by my hood[39] a gentle,[40] and no Jew.

*Lorenzo*  Beshrew me[41] but I love her heartily.

For she is wise (if I can judge of her),

And fair she is (if that mine eyes be true),[42]

55 And true she is (as she hath proved herself).

And therefore like herself (wise, fair, and true)

Shall she be placèd in my constant[43] soul.

ENTER JESSICA

What, art thou come? On gentleman,[44] away,

Our masquing mates[45] by this time for us stay.

EXEUNT LORENZO AND JESSICA

ENTER ANTONIO

60 *Antonio*  Who's there?

*Gratiano*  Signior Antonio?

*Antonio*  Fie, fie, Gratiano, where are all the rest?

'Tis nine o'clock, our friends all stay for you,

No masque tonight, the wind is come about.[46]

65 Bassanio presently will go aboard,

I have sent twenty out to seek for you.

*Gratiano*  I am glad on't, I desire no more delight

Than to be under sail, and gone tonight.

EXEUNT

39 (?) manhood
40 (1) courteous, well-bred, honorable, (2) gentile
41 beshrew me = the devil take me★
42 trustworthy★
43 steadfast, faithful, true
44 spoken to and of Jessica
45 associates, comrades
46 is come about = has turned favorable

## SCENE 7

*Belmont, Portia's house*

ENTER PORTIA AND MOROCCO, WITH THEIR ATTENDANTS

*Portia*  (*to Attendants*) Go, draw[1] aside the curtains, and discover[2]

The several[3] caskets to this noble prince.

(*to Morocco*) Now make your choice.

*Morocco*  The first, of gold, who[4] this inscription bears:

    "Who chooseth me, shall gain what men desire."        5

    The second, silver, which this promise carries:

    "Who chooseth me, shall get as much as he deserves."

    This third, dull lead, with warning all as blunt:

    "Who chooseth me, must give and hazard all he hath."

    How shall I know if I do choose the right?        10

*Portia*   The one of them contains my picture, Prince.

    If you choose that, then I am yours withal.[5]

*Morocco*  Some god direct my judgment. Let me see.

    I will survey[6] th' inscriptions, back again.[7]

    What says this leaden casket?        15

    "Who chooseth me, must give and hazard all he hath."

    Must give, for what? For lead, hazard for lead?

    This casket threatens men that hazard all[8]

1 pull★
2 disclose, show
3 different
4 which
5 as well as/in addition to the picture
6 examine, inspect
7 back again = once again, in reverse order
8 everything

Do it in hope of fair advantages.

20    A golden mind stoops not to shows of dross.[9]

I'll then nor[10] give nor hazard aught for lead.

What says the silver with her virgin[11] hue?

"Who chooseth me, shall get as much as he deserves."

As much as he deserves: pause there, Morocco,

25    And weigh thy value with an even[12] hand.

If thou be'st rated[13] by thy estimation[14]

Thou dost deserve enough, and yet enough

May not extend so far as to the lady.

And yet to be afeared of my deserving

30    Were but a weak disabling[15] of myself.

As much as I deserve: why that's the lady.

I do in birth deserve her, and in fortunes,

In graces,[16] and in qualities of breeding.

But more than these, in love I do deserve.

35    What if I strayed[17] no farther, but chose here?

Let's see once more this saying graved[18] in gold:

"Who chooseth me shall gain what many men desire."

Why that's the lady, all the world desires her.

From the four corners of the earth they come

---

9 dregs, chaff, rubbish
10 neither
11 pure, white
12 steady, uniform
13 evaluated★
14 thy estimation = your own valuation/appraisal★
15 depriving, injuring
16 elegance, refinement★
17 wandered, roamed
18 carved, engraved

To kiss this shrine,[19] this mortal breathing[20] saint.                  40

The Hyrcanian[21] deserts, and the vast wilds[22]

Of wide Arabia are as throughfares, now,

For princes to come view fair Portia.

The watery kingdom,[23] whose ambitious head[24]

Spets[25] in the face of heaven, is no bar                                      45

To stop the foreign spirits,[26] but they come

As o'er a brook to see fair Portia.

One of these three contains her heavenly picture.

Is't like that lead contains her?[27] 'Twere damnation

To think so base a thought, it were[28] too gross                            50

To rib[29] her cerecloth[30] in the obscure[31] grave.

Or shall I think in silver she's immured,[32]

Being[33] ten times undervalued to tried[34] gold?

O sinful thought, never so rich a gem

Was set in worse[35] than gold! They have in England              55

19 container for the relics of a saint (bones, etc.)
20 but still living/breathing
21 Persian
22 wastes, wilderness
23 watery kingdom = ocean, seas
24 ambitious head = swelling foam/froth
25 spits
26 men of spirit
27 i.e., her picture
28 it were = lead would be (though burial in lead caskets was then customary)
29 enclose
30 waxed winding-sheet for a corpse
31 dark
32 enclosed, shut up
33 being as she is
34 to tried = as compared to refined/purified
35 anything worse

A coin that bears the figure of an angel[36]
Stamped in gold, but that's insculped upon.[37]
But here an angel in a golden bed[38]
Lies all within.[39] Deliver me the key.

60 Here do I choose, and thrive I as I may.

*Portia* There, take it prince, and if my form[40] lie there
Then I am yours.

*Morocco* O hell! What have we here,
A carrion Death,[41] within whose empty eye
There is a written scroll.[42] I'll read the writing.

65 All that glisters[43] is not gold,
Often have you heard that told.
Many a man his life hath sold
But[44] my outside[45] to behold.
Gilded timber do[46] worms infold.

70 Had you been as wise as bold,
Young in[47] limbs, in judgment old,
Your answer had not been inscrolled.[48]

36 worth, at the time, roughly half an English pound
37 that's insculped upon = that angel has been engraved (on the coin)
38 i.e., Portia as an angel, here represented by her picture, "asleep" in a casket
39 inside (the casket)
40 image ("picture")
41 carrion Death = a corpse's* skull (known as a "Death's head")
42 paper on which there is writing (often rolled up)*
43 gleams, sparkles, glitters
44 only, just
45 (?) the loveliness that used to be the skull's "outside," (2) the golden surface of the casket
46 does
47 in your
48 written (i.e., it would have been Portia's picture)

Fare you well, your suit is cold.[49]

Cold indeed, and labor lost,

Then farewell heat, and welcome frost. 75

Portia adieu, I have too grieved a heart

To take a tedious leave. Thus losers part.[50]

EXIT MOROCCO

*Portia*    A gentle riddance.[51] Draw the curtains, go.

Let all of his complexion[52] choose me so.

EXEUNT

49 dead
50 depart
51 deliverance (removal, clearing out)
52 (?) (1) nature, temperament, (2) color

## SCENE 8

*Venice, a street*

ENTER Salarino AND Solanio

*Salarino*  Why man I saw Bassanio under sail,

With him is Gratiano gone along.

And in their ship I am sure Lorenzo is not.

*Solanio*  The villain Jew with outcries raised[1] the Duke,

5     Who went with him to search Bassanio's ship.

*Salarino*  He comes too late, the ship was under sail.

But there the Duke was given to understand

That in a gondola were seen together

Lorenzo and his amorous[2] Jessica.

10    Besides, Antonio certified[3] the Duke

They were not with Bassanio in his ship.

*Solanio*  I never heard a passion[4] so confused,

So strange, outrageous,[5] and so variable,

As the dog Jew did utter in the streets.[6]

15    "My daughter, O my ducats, O my daughter,

Fled with a Christian, O my Christian ducats!

Justice – the law – my ducats – and my daughter!

A sealèd bag, two sealèd bags of ducats,

Of double ducats, stol'n from me by my daughter,

20    And jewels, two stones, two rich and precious stones,

Stol'n by my daughter. Justice, find the girl,

---

1 roused (it being night and the Duke in bed)
2 loving
3 assured
4 outburst
5 extravagant, excessive, extraordinary
6 AS the dog JEW did UTter IN the STREETS

She hath the stones upon her, and the ducats.

*Salarino*  Why all the boys in Venice follow him,

    Crying[7] "his stones,[8] his daughter, and his ducats."

*Solanio*  Let good Antonio look he keep his day[9]　　　　　25

    Or he shall pay for this.

*Salarino*　　　　　　　　　Marry, well remembr'd.

    I reasoned[10] with a Frenchman yesterday,

    Who told me, in the narrow seas,[11] that part[12]

    The French and English, there miscarried[13]

    A vessel of our country richly fraught.[14]　　　　　30

    I thought upon Antonio when he told me,

    And wished in silence that it were not his.

*Solanio*  You were best to tell Antonio what you hear.

    Yet do not suddenly, for it may grieve him.

*Salarino*  A kinder gentleman treads not the earth.　　　　　35

    I saw Bassanio and Antonio part.

    Bassanio told him he would make some speed

    Of his return. He answered, Do not so,

    Slubber[15] not business for my sake, Bassanio,

    But stay the very riping[16] of the time,　　　　　40

---

7 calling out
8 (1) jewels, (2) testicles
9 keep his day = meet his contractual day to repay the loan made him by
  Shylock
10 spoke
11 the narrow seas = the English Channel★
12 separate, divide
13 perished, was lost
14 loaded
15 sully, spoil, be careless about
16 ripening, maturation

And for[17] the Jew's bond which he hath of[18] me,

Let it not enter in your mind of[19] love.

Be merry, and employ[20] your chiefest thoughts

To courtship, and such fair ostents of love

45   As shall conveniently become[21] you there.

And even[22] there (his eye being big with tears),

Turning his face, he put his hand behind him,[23]

And with affection wondrous sensible[24]

He wrung Bassanio's hand, and so they parted.

50   *Solanio*  I think he only loves the world for him.[25]

I pray thee let us go and find him[26] out

And quicken[27] his embracèd[28] heaviness

With some delight or other.

*Salarino*                  Do we so.

EXEUNT

17 as for
18 from
19 out/because of
20 use★
21 conveniently become = fittingly/appropriately/properly★ arise/come to
22 right
23 Bassanio (in a kind of affectionate gesture, half embrace)
24 (1) evident, perceptible, obvious, (2) large, considerable, (3) acutely felt, sensitive★
25 for him = because of Bassanio, on Bassanio's account
26 Antonio
27 revive, kindle, rouse up
28 gladly accepted/submitted to

## SCENE 9

*Belmont, Portia's house*

ENTER NERISSA AND A SERVANT

**Nerissa**  Quick, quick I pray thee, draw the curtain straight.
    The Prince of Arragon hath ta'en his oath,
    And comes to his election[1] presently.

ENTER ARRAGON AND HIS ATTENDANTS, AND PORTIA

**Portia**  Behold, there stand the caskets, noble Prince.
    If you choose that wherein I am contained,                    5
    Straight shall our nuptial rights be solemnized.
    But if thou fail, without more speech, my lord,
    You must be gone from hence immediately.

**Arragon**  I am enjoined[2] by oath to observe three things:
    First, never to unfold[3] to any one                         10
    Which casket 'twas I chose; next, if I fail
    Of the right casket, never in my life
    To woo a maid in[4] way of marriage;
    Lastly, if I do fail in fortune[5] of my choice,
    Immediately to leave you, and be gone.                       15

**Portia**  To these injunctions[6] everyone doth swear
    That comes to hazard for my worthless self.

**Arragon**  And so[7] have I addressed[8] me. Fortune now

1 act of choosing
2 commanded
3 disclose, reveal
4 by
5 the luck
6 commands
7 thus, in those terms
8 applied, directed

To my heart's hope! Gold, silver, and base lead.

20 "Who chooseth me must give and hazard all he hath."

You shall[9] look fairer ere I give or hazard.

What says the golden chest? Ha, let me see.

"Who chooseth me, shall gain what many men desire."

What many men desire: that "many" may be meant

25 By[10] the fool multitude that choose by show,

Not learning more than the fond[11] eye doth teach,

Which pries[12] not to th' interior, but like the martlet[13]

Builds[14] in the weather[15] on the outward wall,

Even in the force[16] and road of casualty.[17]

30 I will not choose what many men desire,

Because I will not jump[18] with common spirits,

And rank[19] me with the barbarous multitudes.

Why then to thee, thou silver treasure house.

Tell me once more what title[20] thou dost bear:

35 "Who chooseth me shall get as much as he deserves."

And well said too, for who shall go about[21]

To cozen[22] fortune, and be honorable,

9 must
10 for
11 foolish, credulous
12 looks, searches, investigates
13 bird, also known as a "swift"
14 builds its nest
15 weather-vulnerable conditions
16 vigor, strength, power★
17 road of casualty = way of accident/disaster
18 (1) hop/leap about, (2) agree with
19 stand/classify with
20 inscription
21 go about = endeavor, bestir themselves
22 cheat, defraud

Without the stamp[23] of merit? Let none presume

To wear an undeservèd dignity.[24]

O that estates,[25] degrees,[26] and offices,                    40

Were not derived corruptly, and that clear[27] honor

Were purchased by the merit of the wearer.[28]

How many then should cover[29] that[30] stand bare?[31]

How many be commanded that[32] command?

How much low pleasantry[33] would then be gleaned          45

From[34] the true seed of honor? And how much honor

Picked from the chaff and ruin[35] of the times,

To be new varnished? Well, but to my choice.

"Who chooseth me shall get as much as he deserves."

I will assume desert.[36] Give me a key for this,           50

And instantly unlock my fortunes here.

*Portia*    Too long a pause for that which you find there.

*Arragon*  What's here? The portrait of a blinking[37] idiot

Presenting me a schedule.[38] I will read it.

23 imprint, mark
24 worthiness
25 (1) privileges, positions, (2) means, prosperity
26 rank
27 bright, pure
28 i.e., honor(s) are "worn"
29 gain, make their way, succeed
30 who now
31 (1) stripped of (attainable/possible) prosperity, (2) bare-headed (like servants
   in the presence of masters)
32 who now
33 good humor, facetiousness
34 out of, away from
35 chaff and ruin = rubbish and decay
36 deserving, worth
37 weak-eyed
38 slip of paper

55     How much unlike art thou to Portia!

How much unlike my hopes and my deservings!

"Who chooseth me, shall have as much as he deserves."

Did I deserve no more then a fool's head?

Is that my prize, are my deserts no better?

60  *Portia*    To offend and judge are distinct offices,

And of opposèd[39] natures.[40]

*Arragon*  What is here? (*reading*)

     The fier[41] seven times tried[42] this.

     Seven times tried that judgment is

65     That did never choose amiss.

     Some there be that shadows[43] kiss:[44]

     Such have but a shadow's bliss.

     There be fools alive, iwis,[45]

     Silver'd oe'r,[46] and so was this.

70     Take what wife you will to bed,

     I[47] will ever be your head.[48]

     So be gone, you are sped.[49]

    Still more fool I shall appear

    By[50] the time I linger[51] here.

---

39 opposite, contrasting

40 i.e., he who offends is not in a position to judge what he has done

41 fire

42 refined, purified

43 unreal appearances, delusions

44 there are those who kiss creatures of their own imagining, rather than real people

45 surely, certainly

46 i.e., dressed up by the appearance of merit/worth

47 the "blinking idiot"

48 brain, intelligence

49 dismissed

50 because of

51 have lingered

With one fool's head I came to woo,                    75

But I go away with two.

Sweet, adieu, I'll keep my oath,

Patiently to bear my wroth.[52]

EXIT ARRAGON

*Portia*      Thus hath the candle singed the moth.

O these deliberate[53] fools, when they do choose,       80

They have the wisdom by their wit to lose.

*Nerissa*      The ancient saying is no heresy:

Hanging and wiving goes by destiny.

*Portia*      Come draw the curtain, Nerissa.

ENTER MESSENGER

*Messenger*  Where is my lady?

*Portia*                            Here. What would my lord?[54]      85

*Messenger*  Madam, there is alighted at your gate

A young Venetian, one that comes before[55]

To signify[56] th' approaching of his lord,

From whom he bringeth sensible regrets[57] –

To wit (besides commends[58] and courteous breath),[59]      90

Gifts of rich value. Yet[60] I have not seen

So likely an ambassador of love.

A day in April never came so sweet

52 resentment, wrath
53 careful and slow
54 said in jest
55 in advance
56 indicate, announce★
57 salutations, greetings
58 compliments
59 words
60 before

To show how costly[61] summer was at hand,
95      As this fore-spurrer[62] comes before his lord.
  *Portia*    No more, I pray thee. I am half afeared
      Thou wilt say anon he is some kin to thee,[63]
      Thou spend'st such high-day[64] wit in praising him.
      Come, come Nerissa, for I long to see
100     Quick Cupid's post,[65] that comes so mannerly.[66]
  *Nerissa*  Bassanio, Lord Love, if thy will it be.[67]

EXEUNT

61 sumptuous, extravagant
62 i.e., a "fore-runner" on horseback (using "spurs")
63 i.e., the messenger being less than a "gentleman," so too might the
    newcomer be
64 solemn festival
65 rapid messenger★
66 properly, courteously
67 let it be Bassanio, O Lord of Love, if you so choose

# Act 3

### SCENE I

*Venice, a street*

ENTER Solanio AND Salarino

*Solanio* Now, what news on the Rialto?

*Salarino* Why yet it lives[1] there, unchecked,[2] that Antonio hath
a ship of rich lading wracked[3] on the narrow seas – the
Goodwins,[4] I think they call the place, a very dangerous flat,[5]
and fatal, where the carcasses of many a tall ship lie buried, as    5
they say, if my gossip Report[6] be an honest woman of her
word.

*Solanio* I would[7] she were as lying a gossip, in that, as ever
knapped[8] ginger, or made her neighbors believe she wept for

1 continues to be maintained
2 uncontradicted
3 lading wracked = cargo wracked★
4 the Goodwin Sands, a shoal off the coast of Kent, England
5 shallows, shoals (very broad but having little visible surface)
6 gossip Report = friend/acquaintance Rumor
7 wish
8 nibbled, snapped off (ginger is a root)

10  the death of a third husband. But it is true, without any slips[9]
of prolixity, or crossing the plain[10] highway of talk, that the
good Antonio, the honest Antonio – O that I had a title[11]
good enough to keep his name company!

*Salarino*  Come, the full stop.[12]

15  *Solanio*  Ha, what sayest thou? Why the end is, he hath lost a
ship.

*Salarino*  I would it might prove the end of his losses.

*Solanio*  Let me say amen betimes,[13] lest the divel cross[14] my
prayer, for here he comes in the likeness of a Jew.

ENTER SHYLOCK

20  How now Shylock, what news among the merchants?

*Shylock*  You knew – none so well, none so well as you – of my
daughter's flight.

*Salarino*  That's certain. I for my part knew the tailor[15] that made
the wings she flew withal.[16]

25  *Solanio*  And Shylock for his own part knew the bird[17] was
fledged,[18] and[19] then it is the complexion[20] of them all to
leave the dam.[21]

9 errors, mistaken arguments/inferences
10 (1) direct, straight, simple, (2) manifest, obvious
11 name, rank
12 (1) all right, out with it/say it, get to the end (i.e., to the period in your
   sentence), (2) in horsemanship, suddenly bringing the animal to a stop
13 before it is too late, quickly
14 (1) erase, wipe out, (2) oppose, block
15 (not fanciful: Jessica disguised herself in boy's clothing)
16 flew withal = (1) fled with, (2) flew away on
17 then as now, referring to girls ("bird watching" = watching girls)
18 fully plumed (i.e., grown up)
19 and that
20 disposition, nature (rooted in physiology, as one of the body's "humors")
21 mother* (Is there a wife and mother currently in Shylock's house? We learn,
   in 3.1.103, that her name is or was Leah)

*Shylock*  She is damned for it.

*Salarino*  That's certain, if the divel may be her judge.

*Shylock*  My own flesh and blood to rebel![22]                            30

*Solanio*  Out upon it,[23] old carrion.[24] Rebels it at these years?[25]

*Shylock*  I say[26] my daughter is my flesh and blood.

*Salarino*  There is more difference between thy flesh and hers,
    than between jet and ivory,[27] more between your bloods than
    there is between red wine and Rhenish.[28] But tell us, do you      35
    hear whether Antonio have had any loss at sea or no?

*Shylock*  There I have another bad match,[29] a bankrout,[30] a
    prodigal, who dare scarce show his head on the Rialto, a
    beggar that was used to come so smug upon the mart.[31] Let
    him look to his bond (he was wont to call me usurer), let him      40
    look to his bond (he was wont to lend money for a Christian
    courtesy), let him look to his bond.

*Salarino*  Why I am sure if he forfeit, thou wilt not take his flesh.
    What's that good for?

*Shylock*  To bait fish withal. If it will feed nothing else, it will      45
    feed my revenge.[32] He hath disgraced[33] me, and hindered

---

22 defy lawful authority (a much stronger negative, in Shakespeare's time)

23 you don't mean it!

24 (N.B. the word can also refer to the fleshly nature of human beings)

25 rebels it at these years = does it [your penis] rise up at your age?

26 said

27 jet and ivory = black stone and white ivory (tusks)

28 Rhine wine (white) (these are either comparisons between young blood
    and old, or – literally – between their spirits/essential essences)

29 (1) agreement, bargain, (2) match up, alliance

30 bankrupt★

31 upon the mart = to the marketplace

32 (discussion of Jewish dietary laws, at this point, is irrelevant: no Western
    culture practices cannibalism)

33 degraded, dishonored

me[34] half a million, laughed at my losses, mocked at my gains,
scorned my nation, thwarted my bargains, cooled my friends,
heated mine enemies, and what's the reason? I am a Jew. Hath
50   not a Jew eyes? Hath not a Jew hands, organs, dimensions,[35]
senses, affections, passions, fed with the same food, hurt with
the same weapons, subject to the same diseases, healed by the
same means, warmed and cooled by the same winter and
summer as a Christian is? If you prick us, do we not bleed? If
55   you tickle us, do we not laugh? If you poison us, do we not
die? And if you wrong us, shall[36] we not revenge? If we are
like you in the rest, we will resemble you in that. If a Jew
wrong a Christian, what is[37] his[38] humility? Revenge! If a
Christian wrong a Jew, what should his sufferance[39] be, by
60   Christian example? Why, revenge! The villainy you teach me
I will execute, and it shall go hard[40] but I will[41] better the
instruction.

ENTER A SERVANT FROM ANTONIO

*Servant*   (*to Salarino and Solanio*) Gentlemen, my master Antonio
is at his house, and desires to speak with you both.
65  *Salarino*   We have been up and down to seek him.

ENTER TUBAL

34 hindered me = prevented/stopped me from making
35 measurements, size
36 must
37 is the nature of
38 the Christian's
39 forbearance, toleration
40 it shall go hard = you can count on the fact that
41 but I will = unless/if I do not

*Solanio*   Here comes another of the tribe.[42] A third cannot be
matched,[43] unless the divel himself turn Jew.

*Shylock*   How now Tubal, what news from Genoa? Hast thou
found my daughter?

*Tubal*   I often came where I did hear of her, but cannot find          70
her.

*Shylock*   (*gesturing*) Why there, there, there, there,[44] a diamond
gone cost[45] me two thousand ducats in Frankfort.[46] The
curse[47] never fell upon our nation[48] till now, I never felt it till
now. Two thousand ducats in that, and other precious,          75
precious jewels. I would my daughter were dead at my foot,
and the jewels in her ear! Would she were hearsed[49] at my
foot, and the ducats in her coffin. No news of them,[50] why
so? And I know not how what's spent in the search! Why
thou – loss upon loss, the thief gone with so much, and so          80
much to find the thief, and no satisfaction, no revenge, nor no
ill luck stirring but what lights a[51] my shoulders, no sighs but
a[52] my breathing, no tears but a[53] my shedding.

---

42 loosely used to mean Jews in general (perhaps derived from the 12 original
   tribes of Israel)
43 (?) found
44 (?) there they go?
45 which cost
46 i.e., at a fair, probably the annual jewelry fair, held in the fall
47 (?) possibly Christ's denunciation in Matt. 23:13–39
48 people
49 lying in a coffin
50 Lorenzo and Jessica
51 on
52 of
53 of

*Tubal*    Yes, other men have ill luck too. Antonio as I heard in
85    Genoa –

*Shylock*  What, what, what? Ill luck? Ill luck?

*Tubal*    Hath[54] an argosy cast away, coming from Tripolis.

*Shylock*  I thank God, I thank God? Is it true? is it true?

*Tubal*    I spoke with some of the sailors that escaped the wrack.

90  *Shylock*  I thank thee good Tubal, good news, good news. Ha, ha,
    heard[55] in Genoa.

*Tubal*    Your daughter spent in Genoa, as I heard, one night,
    fourscore[56] ducats.

*Shylock*  Thou stick'st a dagger in me, I shall never see my gold
95    again. Fourscore ducats at a sitting, fourscore ducats!

*Tubal*    There came divers[57] of Antonio's creditors in my
    company[58] to Venice, that swear he cannot choose but break.[59]

*Shylock*  I am very glad of it, I'll plague him, I'll torture him. I am
    glad of it.

100 *Tubal*   One of them showed me a ring that he had of[60] your
    daughter for[61] a monkey.

*Shylock*  Out upon her, thou torturest me, Tubal. It was my
    turquoise, I had it of Leah when I was a bachelor. I would not
    have given it for a wilderness of monkeys.

105 *Tubal*   But Antonio is certainly undone.

---

54 he hath
55 Quarto and Folio "here"; all editors emend, since Shylock is repeating Tubal,
   who said "I heard in Genoa"
56 fourscore = 80
57 various
58 in my company = along with me
59 go under/bankrupt
60 from
61 in exchange for

*Shylock*  Nay, that's true, that's very true. Go Tubal, see me[62] an
officer,[63] bespeak him a fortnight before.[64] I will have the
heart of him if he forfeit, for were he out of Venice, I can
make what merchandise[65] I will. Go Tubal, and meet me at
our synagogue, go good Tubal! At our synagogue, Tubal.  110

EXEUNT

62 see me = see on my behalf
63 constable, sheriff's officer
64 bespeak him a fortnight before = engage him two weeks in advance
65 business

## SCENE 2

*Belmont, Portia's house*

ENTER BASSANIO, PORTIA, GRATIANO,
AND THEIR ATTENDANTS

*Portia*  I pray you tarry,[1] pause a day or two
Before you hazard, for in choosing wrong
I lose your company. Therefore forbear awhile,
There's something tells me (but it is not love)
5  I would not lose you, and you know yourself.
Hate counsels not in such a quality.[2]
But lest you should not understand me well
(And yet a maiden hath no tongue but thought),
I would detain you here some month or two
10  Before you venture for me. I could teach you
How to choose right, but then I am forsworn,[3]
So[4] will I never be, so[5] may you miss me,
But if you do, you'll make me wish a sin,
That I had been forsworn. Beshrew your eyes,
15  They have o'erlooked[6] me and divided me,
One half of me is yours, the other half yours –
Mine own I would say, but[7] if mine, then yours,
And so all yours. O these naughty[8] times
Puts bars between the owners and their rights.

1 delay, wait★
2 (1) frame of mind, character, (2) ability, capacity★
3 breaking my oath
4 that
5 thus
6 bewitched
7 if
8 wayward, wicked★

And so though yours, not yours (prove it so),                    20
Let Fortune go to hell for it, not I.
I speak too long, but 'tis to peise[9] the time,
To etch it,[10] and to draw it out in length,
To stay you from election.

*Bassanio*                                   Let me choose,
For as I am, I live upon the rack.[11]                           25

*Portia*     Upon the rack, Bassanio, then confess
What treason[12] there is mingled with your love.

*Bassanio*  None but that ugly treason of mistrust,
Which makes me fear[13] th' enjoying of my love.
There may as well be amity and life                              30
'Tween snow and fire, as treason and my love.

*Portia*     Ay, but I fear you speak upon the rack,
Where men enforcèd[14] doth speak anything.

*Bassanio*  Promise me life, and I'll confess the truth.

*Portia*     Well then, confess and live.

*Bassanio*                              Confess and love           35
Had been the very sum[15] of my confession.
O happy torment, when my torturer
Doth teach me answers for deliverance![16]
But let me to[17] my fortune and the caskets.

*Portia*     Away then. I am locked in one of them,               40

9 hold suspended/poised/balanced
10 etch it = eke it out
11 a torture instrument
12 breach of faith
13 uneasy/hesitant about
14 forced, compelled★
15 aggregate (total amount/quantity)
16 liberation, rescue
17 go to, seek

If you do love me, you will find me out.
Nerissa and the rest, stand all aloof.[18]
Let music sound while he doth make his choice,
Then if he lose he makes a swanlike end,[19]
45     Fading in music. That the comparison
May stand more proper,[20] my eye shall be the stream
And watery deathbed for him. He may win,
And what is music then? Then music is
Even as the flourish, when true subjects bow
50     To a new-crownèd monarch.[21] Such it is,
As are those dulcet[22] sounds in[23] break of day,
That creep into the dreaming bridegroom's ear,
And summon him to marriage.[24] Now he goes
With no less presence,[25] but with much more love
55     Then young Alcides,[26] when he did redeem
The virgin tribute[27] paid by howling[28] Troy
To the sea monster.[29] I stand for[30] sacrifice,

18 at a distance
19 swans were thought to sing only when they were dying
20 applicable, natural
21 a husband is the lord of a marriage
22 sweet
23 at
24 music was played beneath a bridegroom's window, on the morning of his marriage
25 nobility, dignity
26 Hercules (alSEEdeez)
27 offering
28 wailing
29 The king of Troy, after having hired Poseidon, the sea god, to build Troy's walls, refused to pay him. Poseidon sent a sea monster that could be bought off only if the king sacrificed to it his daughter. Hercules agreed to kill the sea monster if the king gave him the magic horses he owned.
30 stand for = represent

The rest aloof are the Dardanian[31] wives,
With bleared[32] visages come forth to view
The issue[33] of th' exploit.[34] Go Hercules!                    60
Live thou,[35] I live, with[36] much more dismay[37]
I view the sight, than thou that mak'st the fray.[38]

A SONG,[39] AS BASSANIO COMMENTS ABOUT THE CASKETS
                              TO HIMSELF

Tell me where is fancy[40] bred,
Or[41] in the heart, or in the head,
How begot, how nourishèd.                                       65
Reply, reply.

It is engendered in the eyes,[42]
With gazing fed, and fancy dies[43]
In the cradle[44] where it lies.
Let us all ring fancy's knell.[45]                              70
I'll begin it.
Ding, dong, bell.

31 Trojan
32 tear-streaked
33 result, end, conclusion
34 endeavor, enterprise, deed (with connotations of combat)
35 live thou = if you live (i.e., prosper, succeed)
36 and with
37 terror
38 assault, attack
39 (madrigal- or round-like, sung by several voices)
40 amorous inclination ("love," though fancy also can mean whim/caprice)
41 whether
42 it IS enDJENdered IN the EYES
43 can die
44 the eyes
45 funeral bell

*All*      Ding, dong, bell.

*Bassanio*  So may[46] the outward shows be least themselves,

75       The world is still deceived with ornament.[47]

       In law, what plea[48] so tainted and corrupt,

       But being seasoned[49] with a gracious voice,

       Obscures the show of evil? In religion,

       What damnèd error, but some sober brow

80       Will bless it, and approve[50] it with a text,

       Hiding the grossness with fair ornament.

       There is no vice[51] so simple, but assumes

       Some mark of virtue on his[52] outward parts.

       How many cowards, whose hearts are all as false

85       As stairs of sand, wear yet upon their chins

       The beards of Hercules and frowning Mars,

       Who[53] inward searched[54] have livers white as milk,

       And[55] these assume but[56] valor's excrement,[57]

       To render[58] them redoubted.[59] Look on beauty,

90       And you shall see 'tis purchased by the weight,[60]

       Which therein works a miracle in nature,

---

46 so may = even if
47 trappings, decorations
48 suit, action★
49 tempered, fortified★
50 prove, confirm
51 Quarto:"voice"; all editors emend
52 its
53 the cowards
54 examined
55 and yet
56 assume but = put on only
57 dregs, refuse
58 represent, give/make out, show★
59 respected, feared
60 cosmetics and fake hair were purchased by weight

Making them lightest[61] that wear most of it.
So are those crispèd[62] snaky golden locks
(Which maketh such wanton gambols[63] with the wind
Upon supposèd[64] fairness) often known                          95
To be the dowry[65] of a second head,
The skull that bred them in[66] the sepulcher.
Thus ornament is but the guilèd[67] shore
To a most dangerous sea, the beauteous scarf
Veiling an Indian beauty.[68] In a word,                         100
The seeming[69] truth which cunning times[70] put on
To entrap the wisest. Therefore then, thou gaudy[71] gold,
Hard food for Midas,[72] I will[73] none of thee,
Nor none of thee, thou pale and common drudge[74]
'Tween man and man. But thou, thou meager[75] lead               105
Which rather threatnest[76] than dost promise aught,
Thy paleness moves me more than eloquence,

61 most frivolous (pun on body weight)
62 stiffly curled
63 wanton gambols = frisky/unruly/lascivious★ frolicsome movements
64 counterfeited, pretended
65 gift
66 being now in
67 treacherous
68 fair skins then meant: (1) lovely skins *and* (2) light skins, the latter
   nonexistent in India
69 perceived but not real
70 ages
71 showy, brilliant, ornate
72 legendary king who wished that everything he touched might turn to gold
73 want, will have
74 slave (i.e., not everyone could have gold, but silver was "commonly" –
   cheaply – available and used in ordinary coins)
75 lean, scanty
76 (?) because coffins were made of lead

And here choose I, joy[77] be the consequence.

Portia     (aside) How all the other passions fleet[78] to air,

110   As[79] doubtful[80] thoughts and rash-embraced despair,

And shudd'ring fear, and green-eyed jealousy.

O love,[81] be moderate, allay[82] thy ecstasy,

In measure[83] rein thy joy, scant this excess.

I feel too much thy blessing, make it less,

For fear I surfeit.

115 Bassanio              What find I here?

Fair Portia's counterfeit.[84] What demigod

Hath come so near creation?[85] Move these eyes?[86]

Or whether riding on the balls of mine[87]

Seem they in motion? Here are severed[88] lips

120   Parted with sugar breath: so sweet a bar[89]

Should sunder[90] such sweet friends. Here in her hairs[91]

The painter plays the spider, and hath woven

A golden mesh t' entrap the hearts of men

77 may joy
78 drift / float up
79 like
80 ambiguous
81 i.e., the love she feels
82 abate, repress, calm
83 quantity
84 imitation, image ("picture")
85 near creation = close to physical reality
86 move these eyes = do these eyes move
87 balls of mine = my eyeballs (i.e., her eyes appear to move because his eyes move, in seeing them)
88 separated, open, parted
89 obstruction, barrier (her breath)
90 should sunder = must separate
91 hair

Faster[92] than gnats in[93] cobwebs. But her eyes,
How could he see to do them? Having made one,                    125
Methinks[94] it should have power to steal both his[95]
And leave itself unfurnished.[96] Yet look how far
The substance[97] of my praise doth wrong this shadow
In underprizing[98] it, so far[99] this shadow[100]
Doth limp behind[101] the substance.[102] (*picks up paper*) Here's    130
the scroll,
The continent[103] and summary of my fortune.
    You that choose not by the view[104]
    Chance[105] as fair, and choose as true.[106]
    Since this fortune falls to you,
    Be content, and seek no new.[107]                            135
    If you be well pleased with this,
    And hold your fortune for[108] your bliss,
    Turn you where[109] your lady is,

92  more securely, tighter
93  are entrapped in
94  it seems to me
95  both his = both his eyes
96  unsupplied, not provided (with the second eye to match it)
97  matter, thrust
98  undervaluing
99  so far = so far too / equally
100 image (i.e., the painting)
101 limp behind = falls short of
102 reality (i.e., Portia herself)
103 container
104 the view = looking, appearance
105 (verb) it falls out / happens for you*
106 firmly, loyally, trustworthily
107 no new = nothing strange / unfamiliar / additional
108 as
109 to / toward where

And claim her with a loving kiss.

140 A gentle scroll. Fair lady, by your leave,
I come by note[110] to give, and to receive,
Like one of two contending in a prize[111]
That thinks he hath done well in people's eyes,
Hearing applause and universal shout,

145 Giddy[112] in spirit, still gazing in a doubt
Whether those peals[113] of praise be his or no.
So thrice-[114] fair lady stand I even so,
As doubtful whether what I see be true,
Until confirmed, signed, ratified[115] by you.[116]

150 *Portia* You see me, Lord Bassanio, where I stand,
Such as I am. Though for myself alone
I would not be ambitious in my wish
To wish myself much better, yet for you
I would be trebled twenty times myself,

155 A thousand times more fair, ten thousand times
More rich, that[117] only to stand high in your account[118]
I might in virtues, beauties, livings,[119] friends,
Exceed account. But the full sum of me
Is sum of something[120] – which to term in gross,[121]

110 by note = because/by means of what is written (in the scroll)
111 contest, match
112 dizzy, whirling
113 calls
114 triply
115 approved
116 unTIL conFIRMED signed RAtiFIED by YOU
117 so that
118 opinion, reckoning
119 faculties, functioning
120 i.e., nothing in particular/fixed/fully determined
121 term in gross = express/state plainly/bluntly

Is an unlessoned[122] girl, unschooled,[123] unpracticed,[124]  160
Happy in this, she is not yet so old
But she may learn, happier than this,
She is not bred[125] so dull but she can learn.
Happiest of all is that her gentle spirit
Commits itself to yours to be directed,  165
As from her lord, her governor, her king.
Myself, and what is mine, to you and yours
Is now converted.[126] But now[127] I was the lord
Of this fair mansion, master of my servants,
Queen o'er myself. And even now, but now,  170
This house, these servants, and this same myself
Are yours, my lord, I give them with this ring,
Which when you part from, lose, or give away,
Let it presage the ruin of your love,
And be my vantage[128] to exclaim on[129] you.  175
*Bassanio* Madam, you have bereft[130] me of all words,
Only my blood speaks to you in my veins,
And there is such[131] confusion in my powers,
As after some oration fairly[132] spoke
By a belovèd prince,[133] there doth appear  180

122 uninstructed
123 uneducated, untrained
124 inexperienced
125 is not bred = has not been reared
126 turned, changed
127 but now = a moment ago
128 opportunity
129 exclaim on = cry out against
130 deprived
131 the kind of
132 handsomely, beautifully
133 sovereign, ruler, king

Among the buzzing, pleasèd multitude –
Where every something[134] being blent[135] together
Turns to a wild[136] of nothing save of joy
Expressed, and not expressed. But when this ring
185 Parts from this finger, then parts life from hence!
O then be bold to say Bassanio's dead.

Nerissa   My lord and lady, it is now our time
That have stood by and seen our wishes prosper,[137]
To cry good joy, good joy, my lord and lady.

190 Gratiano   My Lord Bassanio, and my gentle lady,[138]
I wish you all the joy that you can wish.
For I am sure you can wish none from me.
And when your honors mean[139] to solemnize
The bargain of your faith, I do beseech you
195 Even at that time I may be married too.

Bassanio   With all my heart, so[140] thou canst get a wife.

Gratiano   I thank your lordship, you have got me one.
My eyes, my lord, can look as swift as yours.
You saw the mistress, I beheld the maid.[141]
200 You loved, I loved. For intermission[142]
No more pertains[143] to me, my lord, than you.

134 every something = every individual thing
135 blended
136 wilderness
137 flourish, succeed, do well
138 Elizabethan audiences would have understood that Bassanio's immense
    new wealth, via Portia, immediately raises his social status and entitles him
    to exactly the deference Gratiano now extends to him
139 propose, plan
140 provided that
141 Nerissa
142 pausing ("delaying") (INterMIseeOWN)
143 applies

Your fortune stood upon the caskets there,
And so did mine too, as the matter falls.
For wooing here until I sweat again,[144]
And swearing till my very roof[145] was dry                    205
With oaths of love, at last (if promise last)[146]
I got a promise of[147] this fair one here
To have her love – provided that your fortune
Achieved[148] her mistress.

*Portia*                            Is this true Nerissa?

*Nerissa*   Madam it is, so you stand pleased withal.          210

*Bassanio*   And do you Gratiano mean good faith?

*Gratiano*   Yes faith, my lord.

*Bassanio*   Our feast shall be much honored in[149] your marriage.

*Gratiano*   We'll play with them the first boy[150] for a thousand
ducats.

*Nerissa*   What, and stake down?[151]                         215

*Gratiano*   No, we shall ne'er win at that sport, and stake down.[152]
But who comes here? Lorenzo and his infidel?[153]
What, and my old Venetian friend Salerio?

ENTER LORENZO, JESSICA, AND SALERIO

*Bassanio*   Lorenzo and Salerio, welcome hither –

144  (?) over and over
145  roof of the mouth
146  endures, holds out
147  from
148  gained, attained
149  by
150  i.e., who has the first boy-child
151  money put up
152  and stake down = if the penis is not erect
153  unbeliever★

93

220   If that the youth[154] of my new interest[155] here
      Have power to bid you welcome. (*to Portia*) By your leave
      I bid my very friends and countrymen,
      Sweet Portia, welcome.

*Portia*                       So do I, my lord,
      They are entirely welcome.

225 *Lorenzo*   I thank your honor. For my part my lord,
      My purpose was not to have seen you here,
      But meeting with Salerio by the way
      He did entreat me past all saying nay
      To come with him along.

*Salerio*                       I did my lord,

230   And I have reason for it. (*gives letter*) Signior Antonio
      Commends him[156] to you.

*Bassanio*                       Ere I ope his letter
      I pray you tell me how my good friend doth.

*Salerio*   Not sick my lord, unless it be in mind,
      Nor well, unless in mind. His letter there

235   Will show you his estate.

BASSANIO OPENS THE LETTER

*Gratiano*   Nerissa, cheer yond stranger,[157] bid her welcome.
      Your hand Salerio, what's the news from Venice?
      How doth that royal[158] merchant, good Antonio?
      I know he will be glad of our success,

154  newness, recentness
155  property rights
156  himself
157  newcomer (i.e., Jessica)
158  splendid, magnificent★

94

We are the Jasons,[159] we have won the fleece.                    240

*Salerio*    I would you had won the fleece[160] that he hath lost.

*Portia*    There are some shrewd[161] contents in yond same
paper,
That steals the color from Bassanio's cheek.
Some dear friend dead, else[162] nothing in the world
Could turn[163] so much the constitution[164]                        245
Of any constant[165] man. What, worse and worse?
With leave Bassanio, I am half yourself,[166]
And I must freely have the half of anything
That this same paper brings you.

*Bassanio*                                    O sweet Portia,
Here are a few of the unpleasant'st words                            250
That ever blotted[167] paper. Gentle lady,
When I did first impart my love to you,
I freely told you all the wealth I had
Ran in my veins, I was a gentleman,
And then I told you true. And yet dear lady,                         255
Rating myself at nothing, you shall see
How much I was a braggart, when I told you
My state was nothing. I should then have told you
That I was worse than nothing. For indeed

---

159 see act 1, scene 1, nn. 170, 171
160 (almost homonymic with "fleets")
161 hurtful, injurious ("very bad")
162 otherwise
163 change
164 disposition, frame of mind
165 steadfast, resolute
166 (i.e., a married couple being a unity, each partner is a half)
167 stained, tarnished

260　I have engaged[168] myself to a dear friend,
　　　Engaged my friend to his mere[169] enemy
　　　To feed my means. Here is a letter, lady,
　　　The paper as[170] the body of my friend,
　　　And every word in it a gaping wound

265　Issuing lifeblood. But is it true, Salerio,
　　　Hath all his ventures failed? What, not one hit,[171]
　　　From Tripolis, from Mexico and England,
　　　From Lisbon, Barbary, and India,
　　　And not one vessel scape the dreadful touch
　　　Of merchant-marring[172] rocks?

270　*Salerio*　　　　　　　　　　　　　Not one my lord.
　　　Besides, it should appear that if he had
　　　The present money to discharge[173] the Jew,
　　　He[174] would not take it. Never did I know
　　　A creature that did bear the shape of man

275　So keen[175] and greedy to confound[176] a man.
　　　He plies[177] the Duke at morning and at night,
　　　And doth impeach[178] the freedom of the state
　　　If they deny him justice. Twenty merchants,
　　　The Duke himself, and the magnificoes[179]

168　obliged
169　downright, entire★
170　is like
171　stroke of good luck, fortunate chance ("success")
172　ruining, destroying
173　fulfill his obligation to ("pay off")
174　Shylock
175　(1) eager, (2) harsh, cruel
176　ruin, destroy★
177　addresses himself to, works at
178　challenge, discredit★
179　the magnates / grandees of Venice

Of greatest port[180] have all persuaded with[181] him,                  280
But none can drive him from the envious plea[182]
Of forfeiture, of justice, and his bond.

*Jessica*     When I was with him, I have heard him swear
To Tubal and to Chus, his countrymen,
That he would rather have Antonio's flesh                  285
Than twenty times the value of the sum
That he did owe him. And I know, my lord,
If law, authority, and power deny not,
It will go hard[183] with poor Antonio.

*Portia*     Is it your dear friend that is thus in trouble?                  290

*Bassanio*  The dearest friend to me, the kindest man,
The best conditioned,[184] and[185] unwearied spirit
In doing courtesies. And one in whom
The ancient Roman honor more appears
Than any that draws breath in Italy.[186]                  295

*Portia*     What sum owes he the Jew?

*Bassanio*  For me, three thousand ducats.

*Portia*                                    What, no more?
Pay him six thousand, and deface[187] the bond.
Double six thousand, and then treble that,
Before a friend of this description                  300
Shall lose a hair through Bassanio's fault.

180 social position
181 persuaded with = tried to convince
182 envious plea = malicious/spiteful* legal action/suit
183 go hard = fare ill
184 best conditioned = best-tempered/disposed/natured
185 and of
186 Italy was the Roman homeland
187 extinguish, wipe out

First go with me to church, and call me wife,
And then away to Venice to your friend.
For never shall you lie by Portia's side
305    With an unquiet[188] soul. You shall have gold
To pay the petty debt twenty times over.
When it is paid, bring your true friend along.
My maid Nerissa and myself meantime
Will live as maids and widows. Come away,
310    For you shall[189] hence upon your wedding day.
Bid your friends welcome, show a merry cheer.[190]
Since you are dear bought, I will love you dear.
But let me hear the letter of your friend.

*Bassanio* (*reads*) "Sweet Bassanio, my ships have all miscarried,
315    my creditors grow cruel, my estate is very low, my bond to
the Jew is forfeit, and since in paying it, it is impossible I
should live, all debts are cleared between you and I, if I might
but see you at my death. Notwithstanding, use your
pleasure.[191] If your love do not persuade you to come, let not
320    my letter."

*Portia*    O love! Dispatch[192] all business and be gone.

*Bassanio*  Since I have your good leave to go away,
I will make haste. But till I come again,
No bed shall e'er be guilty of my stay,
325    Nor rest be interposer 'twixt us twain.

EXEUNT

188  troubled, disturbed
189  (1) must, (2) will
190  countenance, face
191  use your pleasure = do as you think best
192  dismiss, get rid of

## SCENE 3

*Venice, a street*

ENTER SHYLOCK, SOLANIO, ANTONIO, AND THE JAILER

*Shylock*  Jailer, look to him, tell not me of mercy,
This is the fool that lends out money gratis.
Jailer, look to him.

*Antonio*                     Hear me yet, good Shylock.

*Shylock*  I'll have my bond, speak not against my bond,
I have sworn an oath that I will have my bond.                    5
Thou call'dst me dog before thou hadst a cause,
But since I am a dog, beware my fangs,
The Duke shall[1] grant me justice. I do wonder,
Thou naughty Jailer, that thou art so fond[2]
To come abroad[3] with him at his request.                    10

*Antonio*  I pray thee, hear me speak.

*Shylock*  I'll have my bond, I will not hear thee speak,
I'll have my bond, and therefore speak no more,
I'll not be made a soft and dull-eyed fool,
To shake the head, relent, and sigh, and yield                    15
To Christian intercessors. Follow not,
I'll have no speaking, I will have my bond.

EXIT SHYLOCK

*Solanio*  It is the most impenetrable[4] cur
That ever kept[5] with men.

1 (1) must, (2) will
2 foolish, stupid
3 to come abroad = as to come out / away from the jail
4 inscrutable, impervious, impossible (imPEneTRAble
5 stayed, carried on, lodged, remained

| | |
|---|---|
| *Antonio* | Let him alone, |

20     I'll follow him no more with bootless[6] prayers.

He seeks my life, his reason well I know.

I oft delivered[7] from his forfeitures

Many that have at times made moan to me,

Therefore he hates me.

*Solanio*                 I am sure the Duke

25     Will never grant[8] this forfeiture to hold.

*Antonio*   The Duke cannot deny the course[9] of law.

For the commodity[10] that strangers have

With us in Venice, if it[11] be denied,

Will much impeach the justice of the state,

30     Since that the trade and profit of the city

Consisteth of all nations. Therefore go,

These griefs and losses have so bated me

That I shall hardly[12] spare a pound of flesh

Tomorrow, to my bloody creditor.

35     Well Jailer, on. Pray God Bassanio come

To see me pay his debt, and then I care not.

EXEUNT

---

6 useless
7 freed, liberated, saved★
8 agree/consent to
9 force, forward movement★
10 benefit, convenience, advantage ("profit")
11 the course of law
12 barely be able to

## SCENE 4
*Belmont, Portia's house*

ENTER PORTIA, NERISSA, LORENZO, JESSICA,
AND A SERVANT OF PORTIA'S

*Lorenzo*  Madam, although I speak it in your presence,
You have a noble and a true conceit
Of godlike amity,[1] which appears most strongly
In bearing thus the absence of your lord.[2]
But if you knew to whom[3] you show this honor,                    5
How true a gentleman you[4] send relief,
How dear a lover of my lord[5] your husband,
I know you would be prouder of the work
Than customary bounty[6] can enforce you.

*Portia*    I never did repent for doing good,                     10
Nor shall not now. For in companions
That do converse and waste[7] the time together,
Whose souls do bear an egal[8] yoke of love,
There must be needs a like proportion
Of lineaments,[9] of manners, and of spirit,                       15
Which makes me think that this Antonio,
Being the bosom[10] lover of my lord,

1 friendship
2 husband
3 Antonio
4 to whom you
5 man of dignity / stature
6 goodness, kindness, generosity
7 pass, spend
8 equal
9 features, characteristics
10 heartfelt, intimate

Must needs be like my lord. If it be so,
How little is the cost I have bestowed
20    In purchasing the semblance of my soul[11]
From out the state of hellish cruelty.
This comes too near the praising of myself,
Therefore no more of it. Hear other things.
Lorenzo, I commit into your hands
25    The husbandry[12] and manage of my house,
Until my lord's return. For mine own part
I have toward heaven breathed a secret vow,
To live in prayer and contemplation,
Only attended by Nerissa here,
30    Until her husband, and my lord's, return.
There is a monastery two miles off,
And there we will abide. I do desire you
Not to deny this imposition,[13]
The which my love and some necessity
Now lays upon you.

35    *Lorenzo*                    Madam, with all my heart,
I shall obey you in all fair[14] commands.

*Portia*    My people do already know my mind,
And will acknowledge[15] you and Jessica
In place of Lord Bassanio and myself.
40    So fare you well till we shall meet again.

*Lorenzo*  Fair thoughts and happy hours attend on you.

11 (i.e., Bassanio is her soul, and Antonio is the semblance of Bassanio)
12 administration ("running")
13 burden, charge, command (IMpoZIseeOWN)
14 legitimate, reasonable, clear
15 recognize, assent to

*Jessica*    I wish your ladyship all heart's content.

*Portia*    I thank you for your wish, and am well pleased
    To wish it back on you. Fare you well, Jessica.

EXEUNT LORENZO AND JESSICA

    Now Balthasar, as I have ever found thee honest true,    45
    So let me find thee still. Take this same[16] letter,
    And use thou all the endeavor[17] of a man
    In speed to Padua, see thou render[18] this
    Into my cousin's hand, Doctor Belario,[19]
    And look what[20] notes and garments[21] he doth give thee.    50
    Bring[22] them I pray thee with imagined[23] speed
    Unto the traject,[24] to the common[25] ferry
    Which trades[26] to Venice. Waste no time in words,
    But get thee gone, I shall be there before thee.

*Balthasar*  Madam, I go with all convenient speed.    55

EXIT BALTHASAR

*Portia*    Come on Nerissa, I have work in hand
    That you yet know not of. We'll see our husbands

---

16 (?) aforesaid
17 effort, exertion
18 give
19 i.e., not a medical doctor, but a learnèd lawyer
20 look what = make sure that the
21 notes and garments = crib notes as to the relevant laws in Antonio's and
    Shylock's case, which Portia herself knows nothing about, and also the
    barrister robes that must be worn in court (barristers still have "robing
    rooms," in which they change out of their street clothes)
22 you bring
23 all imaginable
24 ferry (Italian *traghetto*)
25 public
26 goes, crosses

Before they think of[27] us!

**Nerissa**                          Shall they see us?

**Portia**    They shall, Nerissa, but in such a habit

60    That they shall think we are accomplished[28]

With that we lack.[29] I'll hold[30] thee any wager

When[31] we are both accoutered[32] like young men,

I'll prove the prettier[33] fellow of the two,

And wear my dagger with the braver[34] grace,

65    And speak between the change[35] of man and boy,

With a reed[36] voice, and turn two mincing[37] steps

Into a manly stride, and speak of frays[38]

Like a fine bragging youth. And tell quaint[39] lies

How honorable ladies sought my love,

70    Which I denying, they fell sick and died.

I could not do withal.[40] Then I'll repent

And wish, for all that, that I had not killed them.

And twenty of these puny[41] lies I'll tell,

That[42] men shall swear I have discontinued[43] school

27 think of = (?) think of seeing
28 equipped
29 (probably a sexual/genital reference)
30 make, offer
31 that when
32 dressed, attired, arrayed
33 most pleasing/gallant/fine
34 more showy, grander, finer
35 variation (i.e., in vocal pitch/range)
36 reedy (hoarse, weak)
37 dainty, elegant
38 brawls, fights
39 ingenious, clever
40 I could not do withal = I couldn't help it
41 inexperienced, raw, novice-like
42 so that
43 left

Above a twelvemonth.[44] I have within my mind                  75
A thousand raw tricks of these bragging Jacks,[45]
Which I will practice.[46]

*Nerissa*                     Why, shall we turn to men?

*Portia*     Fie, what a question's that?
If thou wert ne'er a lewd interpreter![47]
But come, I'll tell thee all my whole device[48]            80
When I am in my coach, which stays for us
At the park[49] gate. And therefore haste away,
For we must measure[50] twenty miles today.

EXEUNT

44 above a twelvemonth = more than a year ago
45 fellows, knaves
46 perform, do
47 Nerissa intends "turn" to mean "turn into"; Portia pretends Nerissa has said "direct ourselves to"
48 plan
49 the grounds / estate surrounding a mansion house
50 travel

## SCENE 5
### *Belmont, a garden*

ENTER GOBBO AND JESSICA

*Gobbo*  Yes truly, for look you, the sins of the father are to be laid
upon the children. Therefore I promise you, I fear[1] you, I was
always plain with you, and so now I speak my agitation of the
matter. Therefore be of good cheer, for truly I think you are
5    damned. There is but one hope in it that can do you any
good, and that is but a kind of bastard[2] hope neither.[3]

*Jessica*  And what hope is that, I pray thee?

*Gobbo*  Marry, you may partly[4] hope that your father got you
not, that you are not the Jew's daughter.

10  *Jessica*  That were a kind of bastard hope indeed, so[5] the sins of
my mother should be visited upon me.

*Gobbo*  Truly then I fear you are damned both by father and
mother. Thus when I shun Scylla (your father), I fall into
Charybdis (your mother).[6] Well, you are gone both ways.

15  *Jessica*  I shall be saved by my husband,[7] he hath made me a
Christian.

*Gobbo*  Truly the more to blame he. We were[8] Christians enow[9]

1 fear for
2 illegitimate, inferior
3 as well, too
4 to some degree
5 in that case, thus
6 Scylla: a many-headed monster; Charybdis: an all-powerful whirlpool;
Odysseus, in Homer's *Odyssey,* was required to steer between the two
7 "For the unbelieving husband is sanctified by the wife, and the unbelieving
wife is sanctified by the husband" (Cor. 1:14)
8 had
9 enough★

before, e'en[10] as many as could well live one by[11] another.
This making of Christians will raise the price of hogs.[12] If
we grow[13] all to be pork-eaters, we shall not shortly[14] have
a rasher[15] on the coals for[16] money.

ENTER LORENZO

*Jessica*    I'll tell my husband, Lancelot, what you say, here he
comes.[17]

*Lorenzo*  I shall grow jealous of you shortly, Lancelot, if you thus
get my wife into corners![18]

*Jessica*    Nay, you need not fear us, Lorenzo. Lancelot and I are
out.[19] He tells me flatly there is no mercy for me in heaven,
because I am a Jew's daughter. And he says you are no good
member of the commonwealth, for in converting Jews to
Christians, you raise the price of pork.

*Lorenzo*  I shall answer[20] that better to the commonwealth, than
you[21] can the getting up[22] of the Negro's belly. The Moor[23]
is with child by you, Lancelot.

*Gobbo*    It is much that the Moor should be more[24] than

10 just
11 (1) next to, beside, (2) off
12 i.e., Jews do not eat pork, but as new Christians they will begin to
13 come ("become")
14 not shortly = soon not
15 fried/broiled bacon
16 in return/exchange for
17 Quarto: come; Folio: comes
18 i.e., tight places (bawdy)
19 unfriendly, quarreling
20 respond to such a charge★
21 Gobbo
22 producing gestation/procreation
23 (rhymes with "more"; the character is not otherwise referred to)
24 bigger

35    reason.²⁵ But if she be less than an honest woman, she is
      indeed more than I took her for.²⁶

      *Lorenzo*  How every fool²⁷ can play upon the word!²⁸ I think
      the best grace of wit²⁹ will shortly turn into silence, and
      discourse grow commendable in none only but parrots. Go
40    in sirrah, bid them prepare for dinner!

      *Gobbo*  That is done sir, they have all stomachs.³⁰

      *Lorenzo*  Goodly Lord, what a wit-snapper³¹ are you. Then bid
      them prepare dinner.

      *Gobbo*  That is done too, sir. Only cover³² is the word.

45    *Lorenzo*  Will you cover³³ then, sir?

      *Gobbo*  Not so sir, neither, I know my duty.

      *Lorenzo*  Yet more quarreling³⁴ with occasion.³⁵ Wilt thou show
      the whole wealth of thy wit in an instant? I pray thee
      understand a plain man in his plain meaning. Go to thy
50    fellows, bid them cover the table, serve³⁶ in the meat,³⁷ and
      we will come in to dinner.

      *Gobbo*  For³⁸ the table sir, it shall be served in.³⁹ For the meat

---

25 reasonably she should be
26 (i.e., I did not think even *that* well of her; "take" also means to possess
   sexually)
27 (Gobbo is a clown/fool)
28 the word = words
29 intellectual sharpness/quickness
30 willingness, appetite★
31 one who makes sharp remarks
32 laying the table
33 Lorenzo does not intend the word to mean, as it can, to put on one's hat, but
   Gobbo so takes it
34 finding fault
35 circumstances, facts
36 bring
37 food
38 as
39 Gobbo deliberately reverses "served in" and "covered"

sir, it shall be covered. For your coming in to dinner sir, why
let it be as humors[40] and conceits shall govern.

EXIT GOBBO

*Lorenzo*  O dear discretion,[41] how his words are suited.[42]        55
    The fool hath planted in his memory
    An army of good words, and I do know
    A many[43] fools that stand[44] in better place,[45]
    Garnished[46] like him, that for[47] a tricksy[48] word
    Defy the matter.[49] How cheer'st thou,[50] Jessica?        60
    And now good sweet, say thy opinion.
    How dost thou like the Lord Bassanio's wife?

*Jessica*  Past all expressing. It is very meet[51]
    The Lord Bassanio live an upright[52] life,
    For having such a blessing in his lady        65
    He finds the joys of heaven here on earth,
    And if on earth he do not mean it,[53] it[54]
    Is reason he should never come to heaven.
    Why, if two gods should play some heavenly match,

40 temperament, mental dispositions ("moods")★
41 dear discretion = heavy-handed making of distinctions
42 sorted out, arranged, adapted
43 a many = many
44 occupy
45 positions/ jobs
46 decked out, dressed
47 for the sake of
48 playful, whimsical
49 substance ("meaning")
50 how cheer'st thou = how do you feel
51 appropriate, suitable, proper★
52 honorable, moral, correct★
53 mean it = intend to live such a life
54 that

70 And on the wager lay two earthly women,
   And Portia one,[55] there must be something else
   Pawned[56] with the other, for the poor rude world
   Hath not her fellow.

*Lorenzo*      E'en such a husband
   Hast thou of me, as she is for a wife.

75 *Jessica* Nay, but ask my opinion too of that?

  *Lorenzo* I will anon, first let us go to dinner!

  *Jessica* Nay, let me praise you while I have a stomach!

  *Lorenzo* No pray thee, let it serve for table talk,[57]
   Then howsome'er[58] thou speakst 'mong[59] other things,
   I shall[60] digest it!

80 *Jessica*     Well, I'll set you forth.[61]

**EXEUNT**

---

55 one of them
56 deposited, pledged
57 table talk = familiar conversation at meals
58 howsome'er = in whatever manner
59 of that among
60 shall be able to
61 set you forth = (1) lay you out (on the table), (2) give you what you
 deserve / need, (3) describe you, (4) praise you, (5) send you away

# Act 4

## SCENE I

*Venice, a court of justice*

ENTER THE DUKE, THE MAGNIFICOES, ANTONIO,
BASSANIO, SALERIO, AND GRATIANO

*Duke*    What, is Antonio here?

*Antonio*  Ready, so please your Grace!

*Duke*    I am sorry for thee, thou art come to answer
    A stony adversary, an inhuman wretch,
    Uncapable of pity, void,[1] and empty              5
    From any dram[2] of mercy.

*Antonio*              I have heard
    Your Grace hath ta'en great pains to qualify[3]
    His rigorous course. But since he stands obdurate,[4]
    And that no lawful means can carry me
    Out of his envy's[5] reach, I do oppose[6]        10

---

1 blank, empty ("ungraced")★
2 any dram = the least weight/liquid contents
3 modify
4 unyielding (obDGUret)
5 (see "envious," in the Finding List)
6 set against

My patience to his fury, and am armed
To suffer, with a quietness of spirit,
The very tyranny[7] and rage of his.

*Duke*  Go one[8] and call the Jew into the court.

15  *Salerio*  He is ready at the door, he comes my lord.

ENTER SHYLOCK

*Duke*  Make room, and let him stand before our face.
Shylock, the world thinks, and I think so too,
That thou but leadest this fashion of thy malice
To the last hour of act, and then 'tis thought
20  Thou'lt show thy mercy and remorse[9] more[10] strange
Than is thy strange apparent[11] cruelty.
And where thou now exact'st the penalty,
Which is a pound of this poor merchant's flesh,
Thou wilt not only lose the forfeiture,
25  But touched with humane gentleness and love
Forgive a moiety[12] of the principal,
Glancing[13] an eye of pity on his losses
That have of late so huddled[14] on his back,
Enow to press a royal merchant down
30  And pluck commiseration of his state
From brassy bosoms and rough hearts of flints,

7 savage severity
8 someone
9 compassion, conscience, pity
10 are more
11 plainly visible, obvious
12 half, part (MOYeTEE)
13 shining
14 piled up

From stubborn Turks and Tartars never trained
   To offices of tender courtesy.
   We all expect a gentle answer, Jew.
*Shylock*   I have possessed[15] your Grace of what I purpose,                    35
   And by our holy Sabbath[16] have I sworn
   To have the due[17] and forfeit of my bond.
   If you deny it, let the danger light[18]
   Upon your charter[19] and your city's freedom!
   You'll ask me why I rather choose to have                    40
   A weight of carrion flesh, than to receive
   Three thousand ducats? I'll not answer that.
   But say it is my humor: is it answered?
   What if my house be troubled with a rat,
   And I be pleased to give ten thousand ducats                    45
   To have it baned?[20] What, are you answered yet?
   Some men there are[21] love not a gaping pig,[22]
   Some that are mad if they behold a cat,
   And others, when the bagpipe sings i'th' nose,[23]

---

15 told
16 "The pious [Jews] in all ages were careful to avoid oaths, especially judicial oaths. . . . [Further, it] is a cardinal rabbinic principle that if a human life is in danger . . . , everything possible must be done even on the Sabbath to save it" (Cecil Roth, ed., *The Standard Jewish Encyclopedia* [New York: Doubleday, 1962], 1441, 1634)
17 debt
18 danger light = loss/harm descend
19 engendering document ("constitution")
20 poisoned, killed
21 are who
22 gaping pig = roasted pig, brought to the table with its mouth either open or containing an apple
23 i.e., nasally

50     Cannot contain their urine[24] – for affection,[25]

    Master of passion, sways it to the mood

    Of what it likes or loathes. Now for your answer.

    As[26] there is no firm reason to be rendered[27]

    Why *he* cannot abide a gaping pig,

55     Why *he* a harmless, necessary cat,

    Why *he* a woolen[28] bagpipe, but of force[29]

    Must yield to such inevitable shame

    As to offend, himself being offended,

    So can I give no reason, nor I will not,

60     More than a lodged[30] hate, and a certain loathing

    I bear Antonio, that I follow[31] thus

    A losing suit against him. Are you answered?

*Bassanio*  This is no answer, thou unfeeling man,

    To excuse the current[32] of thy cruelty!

65 *Shylock*  I am not bound to please thee with my answer!

*Bassanio*  Do all men kill the things they do not love?

*Shylock*  Hates any man the thing he would not[33] kill?

*Bassanio*  Every offense[34] is not a hate at first.

*Shylock*  What, wouldst thou have a serpent sting thee twice?

---

24 *either* (1) their very body revolts at the ghastly sound of the bagpipe, *or*
   (2) the music is so wrenchingly sad that the body as well as the eyes
   weep (cf. act 1, scene 1, n: 61)

25 emotion

26 just as

27 given

28 the bags are wrapped in cloth, when not in use

29 of force = by force

30 established

31 pursue★

32 (1) force, violence, (2) course, direction

33 would not = does not wish to

34 harm, hurt

*Antonio* (*to Bassanio*) I pray you think you question[35] with the     70
> Jew.
>> You may as well go stand upon the beach
>> And bid the main flood[36] bate his usual height,
>> Or even as well use question with the wolf
>> Why he hath made the ewe bleat for the lamb.
>> You may as well forbid the mountain pines     75
>> To wag their high tops, and to make no noise
>> When they are fretted[37] with the gusts of heaven.
>> You may as well do anything most hard,
>> As seek to soften that than which what's harder?
>> – His Jewish heart. Therefore I do beseech you     80
>> Make no more offers, use no farther means,
>> But with all brief and plain conveniency[38]
>> Let me have judgment, and the Jew his will.[39]

*Bassanio* For thy three thousand ducats, here is six.

*Shylock* If every ducat in six thousand ducats     85
> Were in six parts, and every part a ducat,
> I would not draw[40] them, I would have my bond!

*Duke* How shalt thou hope for mercy, rendering[41] none?

*Shylock* What judgment shall I dread, doing no wrong?
> You have among you many a purchased slave,     90
> Which like your asses, and your dogs and mules

35 think you question = remind yourself that you dispute★
36 main flood = (1) high tide, (2) the ocean★
37 agitated, ruffled
38 convenience
39 his will = what he wants
40 take
41 giving

You use in abject[42] and in slavish parts,[43]
Because you bought them. Shall I say to you,
Let them be free, marry them to your heirs?
95  Why sweat they under burthens?[44] Let their beds
Be made as soft as yours, and let their palates[45]
Be seasoned[46] with such[47] viands, you will answer
The slaves are ours. So do I answer you.
The pound of flesh which I demand of him
100  Is dearly bought, 'tis mine, and I will have it.
If you deny me, fie upon your law,
There is no force in the decrees of Venice.
I stand for[48] judgment. Answer, shall I have it?
*Duke*   Upon[49] my power I may[50] dismiss[51] this court,
105  Unless Belario, a learnèd doctor,[52]
Whom I have sent for to determine[53] this,
Come here today.
*Salerio*                    My Lord, here stays without[54]
A messenger with letters[55] from the doctor,

42 degraded, despicable
43 functions, duties
44 burdens
45 taste ("mouths")
46 made savory
47 of the same kind (as yours)
48 stand for = await
49 by means of, in accord with
50 may choose to
51 (it is not clear whether the Duke is considering adjourning the court, to
   await Belario's appearance, or discharging it entirely; the legal procedures in
   the play do not correspond to those of either Venice or Elizabethan England)
52 doctor of law
53 (1) decide, settle, (2) terminate, conclude
54 outside
55 letter

New come from Padua.

*Duke*     Bring us[56] the letters! Call the messengers!       110

*Bassanio*     Good cheer Antonio. What man, courage yet.

    The Jew shall have my flesh, blood, bones, and all,

    Ere thou shalt lose for me one drop of blood.

*Antonio*     I am a tainted wether[57] of the flock,

    Meetest for death. The weakest kind of fruit       115

    Drops earliest to the ground, and so let me.

    You cannot better be employed, Bassanio,

    Than to live still, and write mine epitaph.

ENTER NERISSA

*Duke*     Came you from Padua, from Belario?

*Nerissa*     From both. My Lord Belario greets your Grace.       120

*Bassanio*     (*to Shylock*) Why dost thou whet[58] thy knife so
    earnestly?

*Shylock*     To cut the forfeiture from that bankrout there.

*Gratiano*     Not on thy sole,[59] but on thy soul, harsh Jew,

    Thou mak'st thy knife keen. But no metal can –

    No, not the hangman's ax – bear half the keenness       125

    Of thy sharp[60] envy. Can no prayers pierce thee?

*Shylock*     No, none that thou hast wit enough to make.

*Gratiano*     O be thou damned, inexecable[61] dog,

    And for thy life let justice be accused.

---

56 me (the royal "we")
57 tainted wether = decayed/contaminated castrated ram (bellwether: ram
    with a bell hung around his neck)
58 sharpen
59 i.e., Shylock whets his knife on the sole of his shoe/boot
60 keen, ardent, eager
61 execrable, cursed

130     Thou almost mak'st me waver in my faith,

        To[62] hold opinion with Pythagoras,

        That souls of animals infuse[63] themselves

        Into the trunks[64] of men. Thy currish spirit

        Governed a wolf who, hanged for human slaughter,

135     Even[65] from the gallows did his fell[66] soul fleet,[67]

        And whil'st thou layest in thy unhallowed[68] dam,

        Infused itself in thee.[69] For thy desires

        Are wolfish, bloody, starved, and ravenous.

    *Shylock*   Till thou canst rail[70] the seal from off my bond

140     Thou but offend'st[71] thy lungs to speak so loud.

        Repair[72] thy wit, good youth, or it will fall

        To endless ruin. I stand here for law.

    *Duke*    This letter from Belario doth commend[73]

        A young and learnèd doctor to our court.[74]

        Where is he?

145 *Nerissa*         He attendeth here hard by

        To know your answer, whether you'll admit[75] him.

---

62 and to
63 instill, insinuate★
64 bodies
65 directly
66 savage, ruthless, cruel
67 flow, fly, pass
68 (1) impious, wicked, (2) unconsecrated ("not baptized")
69 i.e., in utero
70 affect/move by cursing
71 violate, wrong
72 set in order
73 recommend
74 to our court = *either* (1) he is recommended to us (as a lawyer), *or* (2) he is
    recommended as someone to join the court, as a judge
75 (1) receive, *or* (2) make him a member of the court

*Duke* With all my heart. Some three or four of you
    Go give him courteous conduct[76] to this place.
    Meantime the court shall hear Belario's letter:
    (*reading aloud*)[77] "Your Grace shall understand, that at the     150
    receipt of your letter I am[78] very sick, but in the instant that
    your messenger came, in loving visitation was with me a
    young doctor[79] of Rome, his name is Balthasar. I acquainted
    him with the cause[80] in controversy between the Jew and
    Antonio the merchant. We turned o'er[81] many books     155
    together. He is furnished with my opinion, which bettered[82]
    with his own learning (the greatness whereof I cannot
    enough commend), comes[83] with him at my importunity[84]
    to fill up your Grace's request in my stead.[85] I beseech you,
    let his lack of years be no impediment to let him lack a     160
    reverend[86] estimation, for I never knew so young a body with
    so old a head. I leave him to your gracious acceptance, whose
    trial[87] shall better publish[88] his commendation."

ENTER PORTIA, DRESSED IN LAWYER'S ROBES

76 escort
77 it is not clear whether it is the Duke or a court official who reads the letter
    aloud
78 was
79 lawyer
80 case, action★
81 turned o'er = read through, searched, perused
82 improved
83 i.e., Belario's opinion comes
84 solicitation, urging
85 (it is not clear exactly what the Duke has requested of Belario)
86 respectful, courteous
87 putting to the proof, testing ("performance")
88 declare

| | | |
|---|---|---|
| *Duke* | You hear the learn'd Belario what he writes, | |
| 165 | And here (I take it) is the doctor come. | |
| | Give me your hand. Came you from old Belario? | |
| *Portia* | I did my lord. | |
| *Duke* | You are[89] welcome, take your place.[90] | |
| | Are you acquainted with the difference[91] | |
| | That holds[92] this present question in the court? | |
| 170 *Portia* | I am informed thoroughly of the cause. | |
| | Which is the merchant here? And which the Jew? | |
| *Duke* | Antonio and old Shylock, both stand forth.[93] | |
| *Portia* | Is your name Shylock? | |
| *Shylock* | Shylock is my name. | |
| *Portia* | Of a strange nature is the suit you follow, | |
| 175 | Yet in such rule[94] that the Venetian law | |
| | Cannot impugn[95] you as you do proceed. | |
| | (*to Antonio*) You stand within his danger,[96] do you not? | |
| *Antonio* | Ay, so he says. | |
| *Portia* | Do you confess the bond? | |
| *Antonio* | I do. | |
| *Portia* | Then must the Jew be merciful. | |
| 180 *Shylock* | On what compulsion must I? Tell me that. | |
| *Portia* | The quality of mercy is not strained,[97] | |

89 you are = you're (for metrical reasons)
90 (?) probably a table set aside for lawyers, in the space in front of the judge and members of the court
91 disagreement
92 keeps
93 stand forth = step forward
94 regulation, force ("principle")
95 oppose
96 power to harm you
97 forced, labored, artificial

It droppeth as the gentle rain from heaven
Upon the place[98] beneath. It is twice blest,
It blesseth him that gives, and him that takes.
'Tis mightiest in the mightiest, it becomes                      185
The thronèd monarch better than his crown.
His scepter shows the force of temporal[99] power,
The attribute to[100] awe and majesty,
Wherein doth sit the dread and fear of kings.
But mercy is above this sceptred sway,                          190
It is enthronèd in the hearts of kings,
It is an attribute to God himself.
And earthly power doth then show likest God's
When mercy seasons justice. Therefore Jew,
Though justice be thy plea, consider this,                       195
That in the course of justice none of us
Should[101] see salvation. We do pray for mercy,
And that same prayer doth teach us all to render[102]
The deeds of mercy. I have spoke thus much
To mitigate[103] the justice of thy plea,                         200
Which if thou follow, this strict court of Venice[104]
Must needs give sentence 'gainst the merchant there.
*Shylock*  My deeds[105] upon my head, I crave[106] the law,

98  i.e., the earth
99  secular, mortal, temporary
100  attribute to = quality/character of
101  would
102  give
103  ease, lessen, abate
104  (it is not clear, still, whether Portia speak *to, of,* or — as a judge — *for* the court)
105  my deeds = let my deeds be
106  demand

The penalty and forfeit of my bond.

205 *Portia*    Is he[107] not able to discharge the money?

*Bassanio*   Yes, here I tender[108] it for him in the court,

Yea, twice the sum. If that will not suffice,

I will be bound to pay it ten times o'er,

On forfeit of my hands, my head, my heart.

210 If this will not suffice, it must appear

That malice bears down[109] truth. And I beseech you[110]

Wrest once[111] the law to your authority.

To do a great right, do a little wrong,

And curb this cruel divel of his will.

215 *Portia*    It must not be, there is no power in Venice

Can alter a decree establishèd.[112]

'Twill be recorded for a precedent,

And many an error by the same example[113]

Will rush into the state. It cannot be.

220 *Shylock*   A Daniel[114] come to judgment, yea a Daniel.

O wise young judge,[115] how I do honor thee.

*Portia*    (*to Shylock*) I pray you, let me look upon[116] the bond.

107 Antonio
108 offer, lay down
109 bears down = overthrows, vanquishes, overwhelms
110 the court, especially the Duke? or Portia, speaking for the court?
111 wrest once = wrench/bend just once
112 decree establishèd = firm /fixed decision/law/statute
113 model, pattern
114 Jewish prophet, exiled to Babylon
115 Balthasar/Portia's exact status seems here to become clearer, though
   Shakespeare's legal arrangements do not completely fit either Elizabethan
   English or Renaissance Venetian law: she is appointed a kind of legal
   arbiter/referee, serving *pro tem* (temporarily) as a judge; this makes at least a
   degree of legal sense (N.B. the editor of this edition is a lawyer and a
   member of the Bar of the State of New York)
116 at

*Shylock*    Here 'tis, most reverend doctor, here it is.

*Portia*     Shylock, there's thrice thy money offered thee.

*Shylock*    An oath, an oath, I have[117] an oath in[118] heaven.          225
   Shall I lay perjury upon my soul?
   No, not for Venice.

*Portia*                        Why, this bond is forfeit,[119]
   And lawfully by this the Jew may claim
   A pound of flesh, to be by him cut off
   Nearest the merchant's heart. Be merciful,                        230
   Take thrice thy money, bid me tear[120] the bond.

*Shylock*    When it is paid according to the tenure.[121]
   It doth appear you are a worthy judge,
   You know the law, your exposition
   Hath been most sound. I charge you by the law,                   235
   Whereof you are a well-deserving pillar,
   Proceed to judgment. By my soul I swear
   There is no power in the tongue of man
   To alter me. I stay here on my bond.

*Antonio*    Most heartily I do beseech the court                   240
   To give the judgment.

*Portia*                        Why, then thus it is.[122]
   You must prepare your bosom for his knife.

*Shylock*    O noble judge, O excellent young man.

*Portia*     For the intent and purpose of the law

---

117 have made
118 to
119 is forfeit = is now in a state of forfeit ("has been forfeited")
120 rip up
121 terms, tenor
122 there is no doubt, here, of Portia's legal status: she speaks *for* the court

245　　　Hath full relation[123] to the penalty,

　　　　Which[124] here appeareth due upon the bond.

　　*Shylock*　'Tis very true. O wise and upright judge,

　　　　How much more elder art thou than thy looks!

　　*Portia*　　(*to Antonio*) Therefore lay bare your bosom.

　　*Shylock*　　　　　　　　　　　　　　　　　Aye, his breast,

250　　　So says the bond, doth it not, noble judge?

　　　　Nearest his heart, those are the very words.

　　*Portia*　　It is so. Are there balance[125] here to weigh the flesh?

　　*Shylock*　I have them ready.

　　*Portia*　　Have by some surgeon,[126] Shylock, on your charge,[127]

255　　　To stop his wounds, least he should bleed to death.

　　*Shylock*　Is it so nominated[128] in the bond?

　　*Portia*　　It is not so expressed, but what of that?

　　　　'Twere good you do so[129] much for charity.

　　*Shylock*　(*examining document*) I cannot find it, 'tis not in the bond.

260　*Portia*　　Come merchant, have you anything to say?

　　*Antonio*　But little. I am armed[130] and well prepared.

　　　　Give me your hand, Bassanio, fare you well.

　　　　Grieve not that I am fall'n to this for you,

　　　　For herein Fortune shows herself more kind

---

123　applicability ("connection, relevancy")
124　the penalty
125　scales
126　physician, medical man (the role we assign to "surgeons," today, was filled by barbers)
127　on your charge = at your expense★
128　designated, specified
129　that
130　ready

Than is her custom. It is still her use                         265
To let the wretched man outlive his wealth,
To view with hollow eye and wrinkled brow
An age[131] of poverty. From which ling'ring penance
Of such miser doth she cut me off.
Commend me to your honorable wife,                              270
Tell her the process[132] of Antonio's end,
Say how I loved you, speak me fair in death.
And when the tale is told, bid her be judge
Whether Bassanio had not once a love.[133]
Repent not you that you shall lose your friend,                275
And he repents not that he pays your debt.
For if the Jew do cut but deep enough,
I'll pay it instantly,[134] with all my heart.[135]

*Bassanio*  Antonio, I am married to a wife
Which is as dear to me as life itself,                          280
But life itself, my wife, and all the world
Are not with me esteemed above thy life.
I would lose all, I sacrifice[136] them all
Here to this devil, to deliver you.

*Portia*    Your wife would give you little thanks for that     285
If she were by to hear you make the offer.

*Gratiano*  I have a wife whom I protest I love,
I would[137] she were in heaven, so she could

---

131  old age
132  events, progress
133  had not once a love = did not once / at one time have a true friend
134  to pay one's death (to nature) = to die
135  all my heart = (1) my entire heart will stop, (2) gladly
136  I sacrifice = I would sacrifice
137  I would = but I wish

Entreat some power to change this currish Jew.

290 *Nerissa* 'Tis well you offer it behind her back,

The wish would make else an unquiet house.

*Shylock* These be the Christian husbands. I have a daughter:

Would any of the stock[138] of Barrabas[139]

Had been her husband, rather than a Christian.

295 We trifle[140] time, I pray thee pursue[141] sentence.

*Portia* A pound of that same merchant's flesh is thine,

The court awards it, and the law doth give it.

*Shylock* Most rightful[142] judge.

*Portia* And you must cut this flesh from off his breast.

300 The law allows it, and the court awards it.

*Shylock* Most learnèd judge – a sentence – come, prepare.

*Portia* Tarry a little, there is something else.

This bond doth give thee here[143] no jot of blood,

The words expressly are a pound of flesh.

305 Then take thy bond, take thou thy pound of flesh,

But in the cutting it, if thou dost shed

One drop of Christian blood, thy lands and goods

Are by the laws of Venice confiscate[144]

Unto the state of Venice.

*Gratiano*            O upright judge!

310 Mark, Jew! O learnèd judge.

---

138 race, ancestry
139 the Jewish prisoner released, instead of Jesus: see Matt. 27:15–26 (BAraBAS)
140 toy with, waste
141 proceed to
142 just, righteous
143 in this writing
144 forfeited

*Shylock*   Is that the law?

*Portia*                     Thyself shalt see the act.[145]

 For as thou urgest justice, be assured

 Thou shalt have justice more than thou desirest.[146]

*Gratiano*   O learned judge! Mark, Jew! A learnèd judge.

*Shylock*   I take this offer then. Pay the bond thrice,   315

 And let the Christian go.

*Bassanio*                     Here is the money.

*Portia*   Soft!

 The Jew shall have all justice.[147] Soft, no haste,

 He shall[148] have nothing but the penalty.

*Gratiano*   O Jew! An upright judge, a learnèd judge!   320

*Portia*   Therefore prepare thee to cut off the flesh,

 Shed thou no blood, nor cut thou less nor more

 But just[149] a pound of flesh. If thou tak'st more

 Or less than a just pound, be it so much

 As makes it light or heavy in the substance,[150]   325

 Or the division of the twentieth part

 Of one poor scruple,[151] nay if the scale do turn

 But in the estimation[152] of a hair,

 Thou diest, and all thy goods are confiscate.

*Gratiano*   A second Daniel, a Daniel, Jew!   330

---

145  law, statute, decree
146  N.B. the distinction between justice (common law) and morality (the law of equity) is in fact made by English law
147  all justice = the whole extent of justice (and nothing else/more)
148  will
149  exactly
150  material (flesh)
151  a very small unit of weight, 1/24 oz.
152  value ("degree")

Now infidel, I have thee on the hip.[153]

*Portia*    Why doth the Jew pause? Take thy forfeiture.

*Shylock*    Give me my principal,[154] and let me go.

*Bassanio*  I have it ready for thee, here it is.

335  *Portia*    He hath refused it in the open court,[155]

He shall have merely justice and his bond.

*Gratiano*  A Daniel, still say I, a second Daniel!

I thank thee, Jew, for teaching me that word.

*Shylock*    Shall[156] I not have barely[157] my principal?

340  *Portia*    Thou shalt have nothing but the forfeiture,

To be taken so at thy peril, Jew.

*Shylock*    Why then the devil give him good of it.

I'll stay no longer question.[158]

*Portia*                  Tarry, Jew,

The law hath yet another hold on you.

345  It is enacted in the laws of Venice,

If it be proved against an alien

That by direct, or indirect, attempts

He seek the life of any citizen,

The party 'gainst the which he doth contrive[159]

350  Shall seize[160] one half his goods, the other half

Comes to the privy coffer[161] of the state,

And the offender's life lies in the mercy

---

153  on the hip = at a disadvantage
154  the sum of the loan, 3,000 ducats
155  open court = publicly
156  must
157  all
158  stay no longer question = wait for no more disputing
159  plot, conspire
160  shall seize = shall be put in possession of
161  privy coffer = the Duke's treasury ("private treasure box")

Of the Duke only,[162] 'gainst all other voice.
In which predicament[163] I say thou standst.
For it appears by manifest proceeding,[164]                    355
That indirectly, and directly too,
Thou hast contrived against the very life
Of the defendant. And thou hast incurred[165]
The danger formerly by me rehearsed.[166]
Down[167] therefore, and beg mercy of the Duke.          360

*Gratiano*  Beg that thou mayst have leave to hang thyself,
And yet thy wealth being forfeit to the state
Thou hast not left the value of a cord.[168]
Therefore thou must be hanged at the state's charge.

*Duke*      That thou shalt see the difference of our spirit,   365
I pardon thee thy life before thou ask it.
For[169] half thy wealth, it is Antonio's.
The other half comes to the general[170] state,
Which humbleness may drive unto[171] a fine.

*Portia*    Ay, for the state,[172] not for Antonio.              370

*Shylock*   Nay, take my life and all. Pardon not that!
You take my house, when you do take the prop
That doth sustain my house. You take my life

162 alone
163 situation, position
164 manifest proceeding = obvious/clear actions/conduct
165 made yourself liable to
166 stated
167 kneel down
168 rope
169 as for
170 whole
171 drive unto = put off/defer/pass/settle into
172 the fine is to be paid to the state, not to Antonio

When you do take the means whereby I live.

375   *Portia*     What mercy can you render[173] him, Antonio?

   *Gratiano*  A halter[174] – gratis.[175] Nothing else, for God's sake.

   *Antonio*   So please my lord the Duke, and all the court

       To quit[176] the fine for one half of his goods.

       I am content, so[177] he will let me have

380      The other half in use,[178] to render[179] it,

       Upon his death, unto the gentleman

       That lately stole his daughter.

       Two things provided more,[180] that for this favor

       He presently become a Christian,

385      The other, that he do record[181] a gift

       Here in the Court of all he dies possessed

       Unto his son Lorenzo and his daughter.

   *Duke*      He shall[182] do this, or else I do recant[183]

       The pardon that I late pronouncèd here.

390  *Portia*     Art thou contented,[184] Jew? What dost thou say?

   *Shylock*   I am content.

   *Portia*              Clerk, draw[185] a deed of gift.

   *Shylock*   I pray you give me leave to go from hence.

173  give
174  rope for hanging
175  free of charge
176  release, remit
177  as long as
178  trust
179  give
180  two things provided more = two more conditions
181  declare, register
182  must
183  withdraw, retract
184  satisfied
185  draw up, write out

I am not well, send the deed[186] after me,

And I will sign it.

Duke            Get thee gone, but do it.

Gratiano   In christening thou shalt have two godfathers.        395

Had I been judge, thou shouldst have had ten more,[187]

To bring thee to the gallows, not to the font.[188]

EXIT SHYLOCK

Duke     (to Portia) Sir, I entreat you with me home to dinner.[189]

Portia     I humbly do desire your Grace of pardon,

I must away this night toward Padua,                  400

And it is meet I presently set forth.

Duke     I am sorry that your leisure serves you not.

Antonio, gratify[190] this gentleman,

For in my mind you are much bound to him.

EXIT DUKE AND ATTENDANTS

Bassanio   Most worthy gentleman, I and my friend           405

Have by your wisdom been this day acquitted

Of grievous penalties, in lieu whereof[191]

Three thousand ducats due unto the Jew

We freely cope[192] your courteous pains withal.

Antonio    And stand indebted over and above             410

In love and service to you evermore.

---

186   agreement of gift
187   i.e., forming a jury of twelve
188   baptismal font
189   sir I enTREAT you WITH me HOME to DINner
190   (1) thank, (2) reward ("pay")
191   instead of which
192   give away in exchange for* which

*Portia*    He is well paid that is well satisfied,

    And I, delivering you, am satisfied,

    And therein do account myself well paid.

415    My mind was never yet more mercenary.[193]

    I pray you know[194] me when we meet again.

    I wish you well, and so I take my leave.

*Bassanio*  Dear sir, of force I must attempt you further,[195]

    Take some remembrance of us as a tribute,

420    Not as fee. Grant me two things, I pray you:

    Not to deny me, and to pardon me.

*Portia*    You press me far, and therefore I will yield.

    Give me your gloves, I'll wear them for your sake,

    And for your love I'll take this ring from you.

425    Do not draw back your hand, I'll take no more,

    And you in love shall[196] not deny me this?

*Bassanio*  This ring, good sir, alas, it is a trifle,

    I will not shame myself to give you this.

*Portia*    I will have nothing else but only this,

430    And now methinks I have a mind[197] to it.

*Bassanio*  There's more depends on[198] this than on the value.

    The dearest[199] ring in Venice will I give you:

    And find it out[200] by proclamation.[201]

    Only for this I pray you pardon[202] me.

193  motivated by money
194  acknowledge, recognize
195  attempt you further = make a further attempt with you
196  will
197  desire, wish
198  depends on = is connected/attached to
199  most expensive
200  find it out = locate the most expensive ring in Venice
201  public notice
202  excuse

*Portia*    I see sir you are liberal in offers.[203]                            435

    You taught me first to beg, and now methinks

    You teach me how a beggar should[204] be answered.

*Bassanio*  Good sir, this ring was given me by my wife,

    And when she put it on she made me vow

    That I should neither sell, nor give, nor lose it.                440

*Portia*    That 'scuse serves many men to save[205] their gifts,

    And if your wife be not a madwoman,

    And know how well I have deserved this ring,

    She would not hold out enemy[206] forever

    For giving it to me. Well, peace be with you.               445

EXEUNT PORTIA AND NERISSA

*Antonio*   My Lord Bassanio, let him have the ring,

    Let his deservings and my love withal

    Be valued against[207] your wife's commandment.[208]

*Bassanio*  Go Gratiano, run and overtake him,

    Give him the ring, and bring him if thou canst             450

    Unto Antonio's house. Away, make haste.

EXIT GRATIANO

    Come, you and I will thither presently,

    And in the morning early will we both

    Fly toward Belmont. Come Antonio.

EXEUNT

203 liberal in offers = generous – but only in what you offer, not in what you
    give
204 must
205 rescue
206 opposed
207 in comparison to
208 injunction, warning

## SCENE 2

*Venice, a street*

ENTER PORTIA AND NERISSA

*Portia*     Inquire the Jew's house out, give him this deed,
And let him sign it. We'll away tonight,
And be a day before our husbands home.
This deed will be well welcome to Lorenzo.

ENTER GRATIANO

5   *Gratiano*   Fair sir, you are well o'erta'en.
My Lord Bassanio, upon more advice,[1]
Hath sent you here this ring, and doth entreat
Your company at dinner.
*Portia*                 That cannot be.
His ring I do accept most thankfully,
10   And so[2] I pray you tell him. Furthermore,
I pray you show my youth old Shylock's house.
*Gratiano*   That will I do.
*Nerissa*            (*to Portia*) Sir, I would speak with you.
(*aside*) I'll see if I can get my husband's ring,
Which I did make him swear to keep forever.
15   *Portia*   Thou mayst, I warrant. We shall have old[3] swearing
That they did give the rings away to men,
But we'll outface them, and outswear them, too.
(*aloud*) Away, make haste, thou know'st where I will tarry.
*Nerissa*   (*to Gratiano*) Come good sir, will you show me to this house?

EXEUNT

1 (1) consideration, (2) counsel, opinion
2 thus
3 abundant, grand

# Act 5

*Lorenzo*  The moon shines bright. In such a night as this,
    When the sweet wind did gently kiss the trees
    And they did make no noise, in such a night
    Troilus methinks mounted[1] the Trojan walls,
    And sighed his soul toward the Grecian tents         5
    Where Cressed lay that night.[2]

*Jessica*                    In such a night
    Did Thisbe[3] fearfully o'ertrip the dew,
    And saw the lion's shadow ere himself,[4]

---

1 climbed onto
2 Troilus was Cressida's true love, Cresseda was Troilus' wandering mistress, in
  both Chaucer's *Troilus and Cresseida* and Shakespeare's 1601–1602 *Troilus and*
  *Cressida*
3 heroine of the tale (retold comically in *A Midsummer's Night's Dream*) of
  *Pyramus and Thisbe:* she drops her cape as she runs; Pyramus finds it, badly
  mauled, and thinks a lion has killed her; he kills himself; she finds him and
  kills herself, too – a typical bit of the blood-and-gore of Ovid's *Metamorphoses*
4 ere himself = moving in front of him

And ran dismayed[5] away.

**Lorenzo**                                        In such a night

10      Stood Dido[6] with a willow[7] in her hand

Upon the wild sea banks,[8] and waft[9] her love

To come again to Carthage.

**Jessica**                                        In such a night

Medea[10] gathered the enchanted herbs

That did renew old Eson.[11]

**Lorenzo**                                        In such a night

15      Did Jessica steal from the wealthy Jew,

And with an unthrift[12] love did run from Venice,

As far as Belmont.

**Jessica**                                In such a night

Did young Lorenzo swear he loved her well,

Stealing her soul with many vows of faith,

And ne'er a true one.

20      **Lorenzo**                                In such a night

Did pretty Jessica (like a little shrow)[13]

Slander her love, and he forgave it her.

**Jessica**      I would out-night you did nobody come,

But hark, I hear the footing[14] of a man.

---

5 frightened

6 queen of Carthage, loved and then deserted by Aeneas, founder of Rome

7 willow branch (symbol of grief for unrequited love)

8 hills/slopes on a sea shore

9 waved, signaled

10 Greek princess and enchantress, who helped Jason capture the Golden
    Fleece but was deserted by him

11 Jason's father, restored to youth by Medea's magic

12 spendthrift, prodigal, shiftless, dissolute

13 shrew, wretch

14 steps

ENTER MESSENGER

| | |
|---|---|
| *Lorenzo* | Who comes so fast in silence of the night? 25 |
| *Messenger* | A friend. |
| *Lorenzo* | A friend, what friend? Your name I pray you, friend? |
| *Messenger* | Stephano is my name, and I bring word |

    My mistress will before the break of day

    Be here at Belmont. She doth stray<sup>15</sup> about    30

    By holy crosses<sup>16</sup> where she kneels and prays

    For happy wedlock hours.

*Lorenzo*               Who comes with her?

*Messenger*  None but a holy hermit and her maid.

    I pray you, is my master yet returned?

*Lorenzo*    He is not, nor we have not heard from him.    35

    But go we in, I pray thee, Jessica,

    And ceremoniously<sup>17</sup> let us prepare

    Some welcome for the mistress of the house,

ENTER GOBBO

| | |
|---|---|
| *Gobbo* | Sola, sola! Wo ha ho, sola, sola!<sup>18</sup> |
| *Lorenzo* | Who calls? 40 |
| *Gobbo* | Sola! Did you see<sup>19</sup> Master Lorenzo? Master Lorenzo, sola, sola! |
| *Lorenzo* | Leave holloaing,<sup>20</sup> man. Here.<sup>21</sup> |
| *Gobbo* | Sola! Where, where? |

15 roam, wander
16 crosses placed in well-frequented public places, for devotional purposes
17 in proper observance
18 an imitation of hunting calls/cries
19 did you see = have you seen
20 leave holloaing = stop making hunting calls
21 here I am

*Lorenzo* Here!

45   *Gobbo*   Tell him there's a post come from my master, with his horn[22] full of good news. My master will be here ere morning, sweet soul.

EXIT GOBBO

*Lorenzo* Let's in, and there expect[23] their coming.

And yet no matter. Why should we go in?

50   My friend Stephano, signify, pray you,

Within the house, your mistress is at hand,[24]

And bring your music[25] forth into the air.

EXIT STEPHANO

How sweet the moonlight sleeps upon this bank.[26]

Here will we sit, and let the sounds of music

55   Creep in our ears. Soft stillness, and the night,

Become the touches[27] of sweet harmony.

Sit Jessica, look how the floor of heaven[28]

Is thick inlayed with patens[29] of bright gold.

There's not the smallest orb which thou beholdst

60   But in his motion like an angel sings,[30]

---

22 post men announced their coming with a horn; Gobbo blends this with "horn" in the sense of a receptacle made of horn, overflowing like a cornucopia or "horn of plenty"

23 await, anticipate

24 at hand = near, close by

25 group of musicians

26 bench

27 playing

28 floor of heaven = the night sky

29 thin circular metallic plates, like tiles

30 i.e., producing, according to this Ptolemaic cosmology, the "music of the spheres"

Still choiring to the young-eyed cherubins.[31]
Such harmony is in immortal souls,
But whilst this muddy vesture of decay[32]
Doth grossly[33] close in it,[34] we cannot hear it.

ENTER MUSICIANS

Come ho, and wake Diana[35] with a hymn!                    65
With sweetest touches pierce your mistress[36] ear,
And draw her home with music.
*Jessica*     I am never merry when I hear sweet[37] music.

MUSIC

*Lorenzo*  The reason is, your spirits are attentive.[38]
For do but note a wild and wanton herd                     70
Or race[39] of youthful and unhandled[40] colts,
Fetching[41] mad bounds, bellowing and neighing loud,
Which is the hot condition of their blood.
If they but hear perchance a trumpet sound,
Or any air[42] of music touch their ears,                  75

31 angels
32 muddy vesture of decay = dirt-garment, mortal and subject (as heavenly
    creatures are not) to decay
33 materially (i.e., with earthly material)
34 close in it = close it in
35 the moon
36 N.B. Elizabethan usage did not require, nor does the Quarto employ, an
    apostrophe to indicate the possessive; addition of an apostrophe would
    negatively affect the meter
37 softly / delicately / gently agreeable / charming / melodious
38 observant, intent
39 stud (a group of animals used for breeding purposes)
40 untamed, not yet broken
41 performing, making
42 (1) breath, sound, (2) melody

You shall perceive them make a mutual stand,[43]
Their savage eyes turned[44] to a modest[45] gaze
By the sweet power of music. Therefore the poet
Did feign that Orpheus drew[46] trees, stones, and floods.
80 Since naught so stockish,[47] hard, and full of rage,
But music for the time doth change his nature.
The man that hath no music in himself,
Nor is not moved with concord[48] of sweet sounds,
Is fit for treasons, stratagems,[49] and spoils,[50]
85 The motions of his spirit are dull as night,
And his affections dark as Erebus.[51]
Let no such man be trusted. Mark the music.

ENTER PORTIA AND NERISSA

*Portia*     That light we see is burning in my hall.
How far that little candle throws his beams.
90 So shines a good deed in a naughty world.
*Nerissa*  When the moon shone we did not see the candle.
*Portia*     So doth the greater glory dim the less.
A substitute shines brightly as a king
Until a king be by, and then his state[52]
95 Empties itself, as doth an inland brook

43 mutual stand = collective stop
44 transformed
45 moderate, orderly
46 attracted
47 stupid, dull ("wooden")
48 harmony
49 schemes, plotting
50 plundering, pillage, rapine
51 a place of darkness, between the world and Hades
52 status, high rank

Into the main of waters. Music, hark.

MUSIC

*Nerissa*   It is your music, madam, of [53] the house.

*Portia*   Nothing is good I see without respect.[54]

Methinks it sounds much sweeter than by day!

*Nerissa*   Silence bestows that virtue[55] on it, madam.                    100

*Portia*   The crow doth sing as sweetly as the lark

When neither is attended,[56] and I think

The nightingale, if she should sing by day,

When every goose is cackling, would be thought

No better a musician than the wren.                    105

How many things by season seasoned are

To their right praise, and true perfection.

Peace![57] How the moon sleeps with Endymion,[58]

And would not be awaked.

MUSIC CEASES

*Lorenzo*                    That is the voice,

Or I am much deceived, of Portia.                    110

*Portia*   He knows me as the blind man knows the cuckoo,

By the bad voice!

*Lorenzo*                    Dear lady, welcome home!

*Portia*   We have been praying for our husbands' welfare,

---

53 from
54 a connection ("context")
55 power
56 accompanied (i.e., when they are alone)
57 be quiet
58 a beautiful young man, charmed into eternal sleep (though the tale does not
   fully explain why)

Which speed[59] we hope the better for our words.
Are they returned?

115 *Lorenzo*                    Madam, they are not yet:
But there is come a messenger before
To signify their coming.

*Portia*                         Go in, Nerissa,
Give order to my servants, that they take
No note at all of our being absent hence,

120 Nor you, Lorenzo – Jessica, nor you.

A TUCKET[60] SOUNDS

*Lorenzo*   Your husband is at hand, I hear his trumpet.
We are no telltales, madam, fear you not.

*Portia*     This night methinks is but the daylight sick,
It looks a little paler, 'tis a day,

125 Such as the day is when the sun is hid.

ENTER BASSANIO, ANTONIO, GRATIANO, AND ATTENDANTS

*Bassanio*   We should hold day[61] with the Antipodes,[62]
If you would walk in absence of the sun.

*Portia*     Let me give light, but let me not be light,
For a light wife doth make a heavy husband,

130 And[63] never be Bassanio so for me.
But God sort[64] all. You are welcome home, my lord.

---

59 prosper, succeed
60 trumpet flourish
61 should hold day = would be matching our sequence of day and night with
   that in the Antipodes
62 those who live on the opposite side of the earth
63 and may
64 dispose, ordain, order

*Bassanio*  I thank you, madam. Give welcome to my friend,
 This is the man, this is Antonio,
 To whom I am so infinitely bound.

*Portia* You should in all sense[65] be much bound to him,  135
 For as I hear he was much bound[66] for you.

*Antonio*  No more than I am well acquitted[67] of.

*Portia* Sir, you are very welcome to our house.
 It must appear in other ways than words,
 Therefore I scant this breathing[68] courtesy.  140

*Gratiano*  (*to Nerissa*) By yonder moon I swear you do me
 wrong.
 In faith, I gave it to the judge's clerk.
 Would he were gelt[69] that had it for my part,
 Since you do take it, love, so much at heart.

*Portia* A quarrel, ho, already! What's the matter?  145

*Gratiano*  About a hoop[70] of gold, a paltry[71] ring
 That she did give me, whose poesy[72] was
 For all the world like cutlers'[73] poetry
 Upon a knife: "love me, and leave me not."

*Nerissa* What talk you of the poesy or the value?  150
 You swore to me when I did give it you
 That you would wear it till the hour of death,
 And that it should lie with you in your grave.

65 good sense, reason
66 put in jail
67 discharged (1) of debt/offense, (2) from jail
68 breath-taxing ("merely verbal")
69 gelded, castrated
70 circular band
71 petty, insignificant
72 brief inscription, engraved motto
73 dealers in/makers of knives

Though not for me,[74] yet for your vehement oaths
155    You should have been respective[75] and have kept it.
Gave it a[76] judge's clerk! But well I know
The clerk will ne'er wear hair on's face that had it.

*Gratiano*  He will, and if he live to be a man.

*Nerissa*    Aye, if a woman live to be a man.

160  *Gratiano*  Now by this hand I gave it to a youth,
A kind of boy, a little scrubbèd[77] boy
No higher then thyself, the judge's clerk,
A prating[78] boy that begged it as a fee.
I could not for my heart deny it him.

165  *Portia*    You were to blame, I must be plain with you,
To part so slightly[79] with your wife's first gift,
A thing stuck on with oaths upon your finger,
And so riveted with faith unto your flesh.
I gave my love a ring, and made him swear
170    Never to part with it, and here he stands.
I dare be sworn for him, he would not leave it,
Nor pluck it from his finger, for the wealth
That the world masters. Now in faith, Gratiano,
You give your wife too unkind a cause of grief,
175    And 'twere to[80] me I should be mad at it.

*Bassanio* *(aside)* Why, I were best to cut my left hand off,
And swear I lost the ring defending it.

74 for me = on my account
75 considerate, regardful, careful
76 to a
77 small, insignificant
78 chattering
79 carelessly, indifferently, easily
80 'twere to = if it were

*Gratiano*  My Lord Bassanio gave his ring away
    Unto the judge that begged it, and indeed
    Deserved[81] it too. And then the boy his clerk,       180
    That took some pains in writing, he begged mine,
    And neither man nor master would take aught
    But the two rings.
*Portia*                What ring gave you, my lord?
    Not that I hope which you received of me.
*Bassanio*  If I could add a lie unto a fault,       185
    I would deny it. But you see my finger
Hath not the ring upon it, it is gone.
*Portia*    Even so void is your false heart of truth.
    By heaven I will ne'er come in your bed
    Until I see the ring.                190
*Nerissa*   *(to Gratiano)* Nor I in yours, till I again see mine.
*Bassanio*  Sweet Portia,
    If you did know to whom I gave the ring,
    If you did know for whom I gave the ring,
    And would conceive[82] for what I gave the ring,     195
    And how unwillingly I left the ring,
    When naught would be accepted but the ring,
    You would abate the strength of your displeasure!
*Portia*    If you had known the virtue of the ring,
    Or half her worthiness that gave the ring,      200
    Or your own honor[83] to contain[84] the ring,
    You would not then have parted with the ring.

81 who deserved
82 think, imagine
83 allegiance, word of honor, conscience
84 hold, keep

What man is there so much unreasonable,
If you had pleased to have defended it
205 With any terms of zeal,[85] wanted[86] the modesty
To urge[87] the thing held[88] as a ceremony?[89]
Nerissa teaches me what to believe.
I'll die for't,[90] but some woman had the ring!
*Bassanio* No, by mine honor, madam, by my soul
210 No woman had it, but a civil[91] doctor,
Which did refuse three thousand ducats of[92] me,
And begged the ring, the which I did deny him,
And suffered him to go[93] displeased away,
Even he that had held up[94] the very life
215 Of my dear friend. What should I say, sweet lady?
I was enforced to send it after him.
I was beset[95] with shame and courtesy,
My honor would not let ingratitude
So much besmear it. Pardon me, good lady,
220 And by these blessèd candles of the night,[96]
Had you been there, I think you would have begged
The ring of[97] me, to give the worthy doctor!

85 fervor, devotion
86 or would have lacked
87 urge that
88 be kept
89 solemnity, something sacred
90 die for't = bet my life on it
91 (1) secular (as opposed to religious), (2) legal (as opposed to medical)
92 from
93 suffered him to go = submitted to/allowed/tolerated his going
94 held up = preserved, sustained, supported
95 surrounded, besieged, assailed
96 i.e., the stars
97 from

*Portia*    Let not that doctor e'er come near my house,
Since he hath got the jewel that I loved,
And that which you did swear to keep for me.      225
I will become as liberal as you,
I'll not deny him any thing I have,
No, not my body, nor my husband's bed.
Know[98] him I shall, I am well sure of it.
Lie not a night from[99] home. Watch me like Argos![100]      230
If you do not, if I be left alone,
Now by mine honor (which is yet mine own),
I'll have the doctor for my bedfellow.

*Nerissa*    And I his clerk. Therefore be well advised
How you do leave me to mine own protection.[101]      235

*Gratiano*    Well, do you so. Let not me take[102] him then,
For if I do, I'll mar the young clerk's pen.[103]

*Antonio*    I am th' unhappy subject of these quarrels.

*Portia*    Sir, grieve not you, you are welcome notwithstanding.

*Bassanio*    Portia, forgive me this enforcèd wrong,      240
And in the hearing of these many friends
I swear to thee, even by thine own fair eyes
Wherein I see myself.

*Portia*                Mark you but that?
In both my eyes he doubly sees himself!
In each eye one, swear by your double self,      245

---

  98  (1) be acquainted with, (2) have carnal/sexual knowledge of
  99  away from
100  shepherd with eyes all over his body
101  to mine own protection = to protect myself
102  catch
103  penis

And there's an oath of credit.[104]

*Bassanio*                                        Nay, but hear me.

Pardon this fault, and by my soul I swear

I never more will break an oath with thee.

*Antonio*   I once did lend my body for thy wealth,

250   Which but for him that had your husband's ring

Had quite miscarried. I dare be bound again,

My soul[105] upon the forfeit, that your lord

Will never more break faith advisedly.[106]

*Portia*     Then you shall be his surety. (*hands him the ring*) Give

him this,

255   And bid him keep it better than the other.

*Antonio*   Here, Lord Bassanio, swear to keep this ring.

*Bassanio*   By heaven it is the same I gave the doctor!

*Portia*     I had it of him. Pardon, Bassanio,

For by this ring the doctor lay with me.

260 *Nerissa*    And pardon me, my gentle Gratiano,

For that same scrubbèd boy, the doctor's clerk,

In lieu of this last night did lie with me.

*Gratiano*   Why this is like the mending of highways

In summer, where the ways are fair[107] enough.

265   What, are we cuckolds[108] ere we have deserved it?

*Portia*     Speak not so grossly,[109] you are all amazed.[110]

Here is a letter, read it at your leisure,

104  of credit = to be believed
105  i.e., that which is infinitely more valuable than his body
106  knowingly, intentionally
107  reputable, good
108  the deceived husbands of unfaithful wives
109  excessively
110  bewildered, confused

It comes from Padua,[111] from Belario.
There you shall find that Portia was the doctor,
Nerissa there her clerk. Lorenzo here                                    270
Shall witness I set forth as soon as you,
And but e'en now returned. I have not yet
Entered my house. Antonio, you are welcome,
And I have better news in store for you
Than you expect. Unseal this letter soon,                                275
There you shall find[112] three of your argosies
Are richly[113] come to harbor suddenly.[114]
You shall not know by what strange accident
I chancèd on this letter.

Antonio                              I am dumb.

Bassanio  Were you the doctor, and I knew you not?          280

Gratiano  Were you the clerk that is to make me cuckold?

Nerissa    Aye, but the clerk that never means to do it –
Unless he live until he be a man.

Bassanio  Sweet doctor, you shall be my bedfellow.
When I am absent, then lie with my wife.                                285

Antonio   Sweet lady, you have given me life and living,
For here I read for certain that my ships
Are safely come to road.[115]

Portia                              How now, Lorenzo?
My clerk hath some good comforts,[116] too, for you.

Nerissa    Aye, and I'll give them him without a fee.                 290

111 PAdyooAH
112 learn/discover that
113 splendidly, wealthily
114 unexpectedly
115 sheltered water near a harbor
116 pleasures, delights

There do I give to you and Jessica,

From the rich Jew, a special deed of gift,

After his death, of all he dies possessed of.

*Lorenzo*  Fair ladies, you drop manna[117] in the way

Of starvèd people.

295 *Portia*                    It is almost morning,

And yet I am sure you are not satisfied

Of these events at full.[118] Let us go in,

And charge us[119] there upon interrogatories,[120]

And we will answer all things faithfully.

300 *Gratiano*  Let it be so. The first interrogatory

That my Nerissa shall be sworn on is

Whether till the next night she had rather stay,[121]

Or go to bed, now being two hours to[122] day.

But were the day come, I should wish it dark,

305        Till I were couching[123] with the doctor's clerk.[124]

Well, while I live I'll fear no other thing

So sore,[125] as keeping safe Nerissa's ring.[126]

EXEUNT

117 food dropped from heaven, to feed the starving Israelites after they left
Egypt and were in the barren desert (Exod. 16)
118 at full = completely
119 charge us = put us on oath, as in a courtroom
120 formal questioning
121 wait
122 till
123 lying down (in bed)
124 "clerk" in British English is to this day pronounced "clark"
125 seriously
126 bawdy pun on female genitalia

S hylock is to the world of the comedies and romances what Hamlet is to the tragedies, and Falstaff to the histories: a representation so original as to be perpetually bewildering to us. What is beyond us in Hamlet and Falstaff is a mode of vast consciousness crossed by wit, so that we know authentic disinterestedness only by knowing the Hamlet of act 5, and know the wit that enlarges existence best by knowing Falstaff before his rejection by King Henry V, who has replaced Hal. Shylock is not beyond us in any way, and yet he resembles Hamlet and Falstaff in one crucial regard: he is a much more problematical representation than even Shakespeare's art could have intended. Like Hamlet and Falstaff, he dwarfs his fellow characters. Portia, despite her aura, fades before him just as Claudius recedes in the clash of might opposites with Hamlet, and as Hotspur is dimmed by Falstaff.

I know of no legitimate way in which *The Merchant of Venice* ought to be regarded as other than an anti-Semitic text, agreeing in this with E. E. Stoll as against Harold Goddard, my favorite critic of Shakespeare. Goddard sees Antonio and Portia as self-betrayers, who should have done better. They seem to me perfectly adequate Christians, with Antonio's anti-Semitism being rather less judicious than Portia's, whose attitude approximates that of the T. S. Eliot of *After Strange Gods, The Idea of a Christian Society,* and the earlier poems. If you accept the attitude towards the Jews of the Gospel of John, then you will behave towards Shylock as Portia does, or as Eliot doubtless would have behaved towards British Jewry, had the Nazis defeated and occupied Eliot's adopted country. To Portia, and to Eliot, the Jews were what they are called in the Gospel of John: descendants of Satan, rather than of Abraham.

There is no real reason to doubt that the historical Shakespeare would have agreed with his Portia. Shakespeare after all wrote what might as well be called *The Jew of Venice,* in clear rivalry with his precursor Marlowe's *The Jew of Malta.* Were I an actor, I would take great pleasure in the part of Barabas, and little or none in that of Shylock, but then I am a Jewish critic, and prefer the exuberance of Barabas to the wounded intensity of Shylock. There is nothing problematic about Barabas. We cannot imagine *him* asking: "If you prick us, do we not bleed?" any more than we can imagine Shylock proclaiming: "As for myself, I walk abroad a-nights . . . and poison wells." Marlowe, subtly blasphemous and cunningly outrageous, gives us Christians and Muslims who are as reprehensible as Barabas, but who lack the Jew of Malta's superb delight in his own sublime villainy. Despite his moralizing scholars, Marlowe the poet is Barabas, or rhetorically so akin to his creation as to render the difference uninteresting. Shakespeare possibly intended to give us a pathetic monster in Shylock, but being Shakespeare, he gave us Shylock, concerning whom little can be said that will not be at least oxymoronic, if not indeed self-contradictory.

That Shylock got away from Shakespeare seems clear enough, but that is the scandal of Shakespearean representation; so strong is it that nearly all his creatures break out of the temporal trap of Elizabethan and Jacobean mimesis, and establish standards of imitation that do seem to be, not of an age, but for all time. Shylock also—like Hamlet, Falstaff, Cleopatra—compels us to see differences in reality we otherwise could not have seen. Marlowe is a great caricaturist; Barabas is grotesquely magnificent, and his extravagance mocks the Christian cartoon of the Jew as usurer and fiend. It hardly matters whether the mockery is involuntary, since inevitably the hyperbolic force of the Marlovian rhetoric raises word-consciousness to a level where everything joins in an overreaching. In a cosmos where all is excessive, Barabas is no more a Jew than Tamburlaine is a Scythian or Faustus a Christian. It is much more troublesome to ask, Is Shylock a Jew? Does he not now represent something our culture regards as being essentially Jewish? So immense is the power of Shakespearean mimesis that its capacity for harm necessarily might be as substantial as its enabling force has been for augmenting cognition and for fostering psychoanalysis, despite all Freud's anxious assertions of his own originality.

Harold Goddard, nobly creating a Shakespeare in his own highly humane image, tried to persuade himself "that Shakespeare planned his play from the outset to enforce the irony of Portia's failure to be true to her inner self in the trial scene." E. E. Stoll, sensibly declaring that Shakespeare's contemporary audience set societal limits that Shakespeare himself would not have thought to transcend, reminds us that Jew-baiting was in effect little different from bear-baiting for that audience. I do not hope for a better critic of Shakespeare than Goddard. Like Freud, Goddard always looked for what Shakespeare shared with Dostoevsky, which seems to me rather more useful than searching for what Shakespeare shared with Kyd or even with Marlowe or Webster. Despite his authentic insistence that Shakespeare always was poet as well as playwright, Goddard's attempt to see *The Merchant of Venice* as other than anti-Semitic was misguided.

At his very best, Goddard antithetically demonstrates that the play's "spiritual argument" is quite simply unacceptable to us now:

> Shylock's conviction that Christianity and revenge are synonyms is confirmed. "If a Christian wrong a Jew, what should his sufferance be by Christian example? Why, revenge." The unforgettable speech from which that comes, together with Portia's on mercy, and Lorenzo's on the harmony of heaven, make up the spiritual argument of the play. Shylock asserts that a Jew is a man. Portia declares that man's duty to man is mercy—which comes from heaven. Lorenzo points to heaven but laments that the materialism of life insulates man from its harmonies. A celestial syllogism that puts to shame the logic of the courtroom.

Alas, the celestial syllogism is Goddard's, and Portia's logic is Shakespeare's. Goddard wanted to associate *The Merchant of Venice* with Chekhov's bittersweet "Rothschild's Fiddle," but Dostoevsky again would have been the right comparison. Shakespeare's indubitable anti-Semitism is no lovelier than Dostoevsky's, being compounded similarly out of xenophobia and the Gospel of John. Shylock's demand for justice, as contrasted to Portia's supposed mercy, is part of the endless consequence of the New Testament's slander against the Pharisees. But the authors of the New Testament, even Paul and John, were no match for the authors of the Hebrew Bible. Shakespeare, more even than Dostoevsky, is of another order, the order of the Yahwist, Homer, Dante, Chaucer, Cervantes, Tolstoy—the great masters of Western literary representation. Shylock is essentially a comic representation rendered something other than comic because of Shakespeare's preternatural ability to accomplish a super-mimesis of essential nature. Shakespeare's intellectual, Hamlet, is necessarily the paradigm of *the* intellectual, even as Falstaff is the model of wit, and Cleopatra the sublime of eros. Is Shakespeare's Jew fated to go on being the representation of *the* Jew?

"Yes and no," would be my answer, because of Shakespeare's own partial failure when he allows Shylock to invoke an even stronger representation of *the* Jew, the Yahwist's vision of the superbly tenacious Jacob tending the flocks of Laban and not directly taking interest. Something very odd is at work when Antonio denies Jacob's own efficacy:

> This was a venture, sir, that Jacob served for,
> A thing not in his power to bring to pass,
> But swayed and fashioned by the hand of heaven.
>
> (1.3.85–87)

That is certainly a Christian reading, though I do not assert necessarily it was Shakespeare's own. Good Christian merchant that he is, Antonio distinguishes his own profits from Shylock's Jewish usury, but Shylock, or rather the Yahwist, surely wins the point over Antonio, and perhaps over Shakespeare. If the Jewish "divel can cite Scripture for his purpose," so can the Christian devils, from John through Shakespeare, and the polemical point turns upon who wins the agon, the Yahwist or Shakespeare? Shakespeare certainly intended to show the Jew as caught in the repetition of a revenge morality masking itself as a demand for justice. That is the rhetorical force of Shylock's obsessive "I will have my bond," with all its dreadfully compulsive ironic plays upon "bond." But if Shylock, like the Yahwist's Jacob, is a strong representation of the Jew, then "bond" has a tenacity that Shakespeare himself may have underestimated. Shakespeare's most dubious irony, as little persuasive as the resolution of *Measure for Measure,* is that Portia triumphantly out-literalizes Shylock's literalism, since flesh cannot be separated from blood. But Shylock, however monstrously, has a true bond or covenant to assert, whether between himself and Antonio, or between Jacob and Laban, or ultimately between Israel and Antonio, or between Jacob and Laban, or ultimately between Israel and Yahweh. Portia invokes an unequal law, not a covenant or mutual obligation, but only another variant upon the age-old Christian insistence that Christians may shed Jewish blood, but never the reverse. Can it be said that we do not go on hearing Shylock's "I will have my bond," despite his forced conversion?

Shakespearean representation presents us with many perplexities throughout the comedies and romances: Angelo and Malvolio, among others, are perhaps as baffling as Shylock. What makes Shylock different may be a strength in the language he speaks that works against what elsewhere is Shakespeare's most original power. Shylock does not change by listening to himself speaking; he becomes only more what he always was. It is as though the Jew alone, in Shakespeare, lacks originality. Marlowe's Barabas *sounds* less original than Shylock does, and yet Marlowe employs Barabas to satirize Christian moral pretensions. The curious result is that Marlowe, just this once, seems "modern" in contrast to Shakespeare. What are we to do with Shylock's great outbursts of pathos when the play itself seems to give them no dignity or value in context? I do not find it possible to contravene E. E. Stoll's judgment in this regard:

> Shylock's disappointment is tragic to him, but good care is taken that it shall not be to us. . . . The running fire assails him to the very moment—and beyond it—that Shylock says he is not well, and staggers out, amid Gratiano's jeers touching his baptism, to provoke in the audience the laughter of triumph and vengeance in his own day and bring tears to their eyes in ours. How can we here for a moment sympathize with Shylock unless at the same time we indignantly turn, not only against Gratiano, but against Portia, the Duke, and all Venice as well?

We cannot, unless we desire to read or see some other play. *The Merchant of Venice* demands what we cannot accept: Antonio's superior goodness, from the start, is to be demonstrated by his righteous scorn for Shylock, which is to say, Antonio most certainly represents what now is called a Jew-baiter. An honest production of the play, sensitive to its values, would now be intolerable in a Western country. The unhappy paradox is that *The Jew of Malta,* a ferocious farce, exposes the madness and hypocrisy of Jew-baiting, even though its Machiavel, Barabas, is the Jewish monster or Devil incarnate, while *The Merchant of Venice* is at once a comedy of delightful sophistication and a vicious Christian slander against the Jews.

In that one respect, Shakespeare was of an age, and not for all time. Bardolatry is not always an innocent disease, and produces odd judgments, as when J. Middleton Murry insisted: "*The Merchant of Venice* is not a problem play; it is a fairy story." For us, contemporary Jews and Gentiles alike, it had better be a problem play, and not a fairy story. Shylock, Murry admitted, was not "coherent," because a Shakespearean character had no need to be coherent. Yet Shylock is anything but incoherent. His palpable mimetic force enhances his rapacity and viciousness, and works to make an ancient bogeyman come dreadfully alive. For the reader or playgoer (though hardly the latter, in our time), Shylock is at once comic and frightening, a walking embodiment of the death drive.

We must not underestimate the power and influence of Shakespearean mimesis, even when it is *deliberately* unoriginal, as it is in Shylock. Hamlet and Falstaff contain us to our enrichment. Shylock has the strength to contain us to our destruction. Something of the same could be said for Angelo, in *Measure for Measure,* or of Malvolio, in *Twelfth Night,* or of nearly everyone in *Troilus.* History renders Shylock's strength as representation socially destructive, whereas Angelo and Malvolio inhabit the shadows of the individual consciousness. I conclude by noting that Shakespeare's comedies and romances share in the paradox that Gershom Scholem said the writings of Kafka possessed. They have for us "something of the strong light of the canonical, of the perfection that destroys."

# FURTHER READING

This is not a bibliography but a selective set of starting places.

## Texts

Shakespeare, William. *The First Folio of Shakespeare,* 2d ed. Edited by
    Charlton Hinman. Introduction by Peter W. M. Blayney. New York:
    W. W. Norton, 1996.
———. *The Merchant of Venice, the Old-Spelling Shakespeare* [1600
    Quarto] . . . . New York: Duffield, 1909.

## Language

Dobson, E. J. *English Pronunciation, 1500–1700.* 2d ed. Oxford: Oxford
    University Press, 1968.
Houston, John Porter. *The Rhetoric of Poetry in the Renaissance and
    Seventeenth Century.* Baton Rouge: Louisiana State University Press,
    1983.
———. *Shakespearean Sentences: A Study in Style and Syntax.* Baton
    Rouge: Louisiana State University Press, 1988.
Kermode, Frank. *Shakespeare's Language.* New York: Farrar, Straus and
    Giroux, 2000.
Kökeritz, Helge. *Shakespeare's Pronunciation.* New Haven: Yale
    University Press, 1953.
Lanham, Richard A. *The Motives of Eloquence: Literary Rhetoric in the
    Renaissance.* New Haven and London: Yale University Press, 1976.

*The Oxford English Dictionary: Second Edition on CD-ROM, version 3.0.*
   New York: Oxford University Press, 2002.

Raffel, Burton. *From Stress to Stress: An Autobiography of English Prosody.*
   Hamden, Conn.: Archon Books, 1992.

Ronberg, Gert. A *Way with Words: The Language of English Renaissance
   Literature.* London: Arnold, 1992.

Trousdale, Marion. *Shakespeare and the Rhetoricians.* Chapel Hill:
   University of North Carolina Press, 1982.

## Culture

Bindoff, S. T. *Tudor England.* Baltimore: Penguin, 1950.

Bradbrook, M. C. *Shakespeare: The Poet in His World.* New York:
   Columbia University Press, 1978.

Brown, Cedric C., ed. *Patronage, Politics, and Literary Tradition in England,
   1558–1658.* Detroit, Mich.: Wayne State University Press, 1993.

Bush, Douglas. *Prefaces to Renaissance Literature.* New York: W. W.
   Norton, 1965.

Buxton, John. *Elizabethan Taste.* London: Harvester, 1963.

Cowan, Alexander. *Urban Europe, 1500–1700.* New York: Oxford
   University Press, 1998.

Driver, Tom E. *The Sense of History in Greek and Shakespearean Drama.*
   New York: Columbia University Press, 1960.

Finucci, Valeria, and Regina Schwartz, eds. *Desire in the Renaissance:
   Psychoanalysis and Literature.* Princeton, N.J.: Princeton University
   Press, 1994.

Fumerton, Patricia, and Simon Hunt, eds. *Renaissance Culture and the
   Everyday.* Philadelphia: University of Pennsylvania Press, 1999.

Gross, John. *Shylock: A Legend and Its Legacy.* New York: Simon and
   Schuster, 1992.

Halliday, F. E. *Shakespeare in His Age.* South Brunswick, N.J.: Yoseloff,
   1965.

Harrison, G. B., ed. *The Elizabethan Journals: Being a Record of Those
   Things Most Talked of During the Years 1591–1597.* Abridged ed. 2 vols.
   New York: Doubleday Anchor, 1965.

Harrison, William. *The Description of England: The Classic Contemporary*

*[1577] Account of Tudor Social Life.* Edited by Georges Edelen. Washington, D.C.: Folger Shakespeare Library, 1968. Reprint, New York: Dover, 1994.

Jardine, Lisa. "Introduction." In Jardine, *Reading Shakespeare Historically.* London: Routledge, 1996.

———. *Worldly Goods: A New History of the Renaissance.* London: Macmillan, 1996.

Jeanneret, Michel. *A Feast of Words: Banquets and Table Talk in the Renaissance.* Translated by Jeremy Whiteley and Emma Hughes. Chicago: University of Chicago Press, 1991.

Kernan, Alvin. *Shakespeare, the King's Playwright: Theater in the Stuart Court, 1603–1613.* New Haven: Yale University Press, 1995.

Lockyer, Roger. *Tudor and Stuart Britain, 1471–1714.* London: Longmans, 1964.

Norwich, John Julius. *Shakespeare's Kings: The Great Plays and the History of England in the Middle Ages, 1337–1485.* New York: Scribner, 2000.

Rose, Mary Beth, ed. *Renaissance Drama as Cultural History: Essays from Renaissance Drama, 1977–1987.* Evanston, Ill.: Northwestern University Press, 1990.

Schmidgall, Gary. *Shakespeare and the Courtly Aesthetic.* Berkeley: University of California Press, 1981.

Shapiro, James. *Shakespeare and the Jews.* New York: Columbia University Press, 1996.

Smith, G. Gregory, ed. *Elizabethan Critical Essays.* 2 vols. Oxford: Clarendon Press, 1904.

Tillyard, E. M. W. *The Elizabethan World Picture.* London: Chatto and Windus, 1943. Reprint, Harmondsworth: Penguin, 1963.

Willey, Basil. *The Seventeenth Century Background: Studies in the Thought of the Age in Relation to Poetry and Religion.* New York: Columbia University Press, 1933. Reprint, New York: Doubleday, 1955.

Wilson, F. P. *The Plague in Shakespeare's London.* 2d ed. Oxford: Oxford University Press, 1963.

Wilson, John Dover. *Life in Shakespeare's England: A Book of Elizabethan Prose.* 2d ed. Cambridge: Cambridge University Press, 1913. Reprint, Harmondsworth: Penguin, 1944.

Yaffe, Martin D. *Shylock and the Jewish Question*. Baltimore: Johns Hopkins University Press, 1997.

Zimmerman, Susan, and Ronald F. E. Weissman, eds. *Urban Life in the Renaissance*. Newark: University of Delaware Press, 1989.

## Dramatic Development

Cohen, Walter. *Drama of a Nation: Public Theater in Renaissance England and Spain*. Ithaca, N.Y.: Cornell University Press, 1985.

Dessen, Alan C. *Shakespeare and the Late Moral Plays*. Lincoln: University of Nebraska Press, 1986.

Fraser, Russell A., and Norman Rabkin, eds. *Drama of the English Renaissance*. 2 vols. Upper Saddle River, N.J.: Prentice Hall, 1976.

Happé, Peter, ed. *Tudor Interludes*. Harmondsworth: Penguin, 1972.

Laroque, François. *Shakespeare's Festive World: Elizabethan Seasonal Entertainment and the Professional Stage*. Translated by Janet Lloyd. Cambridge: Cambridge University Press, 1991.

Norland, Howard B. *Drama in Early Tudor Britain, 1485–1558*. Lincoln: University of Nebraska Press, 1995.

## Theater and Stage

Doran, Madeleine. *Endeavors of Art: A Study of Form in Elizabethan Drama*. Milwaukee: University of Wisconsin Press, 1954.

Grene, David. *The Actor in History: Studies in Shakespearean Stage Poetry*. University Park: Pennsylvania State University Press, 1988.

Gurr, Andrew. *Playgoing in Shakespeare's London*. Cambridge: Cambridge University Press, 1987.

———. *The Shakespearian Stage, 1574–1642*. 3d ed. Cambridge: Cambridge University Press, 1992.

Halliday, F. E. *A Shakespeare Companion, 1564–1964*. Rev. ed. Harmondsworth: Penguin, 1964.

Harrison, G. B. *Elizabethan Plays and Players*. Ann Arbor: University of Michigan Press, 1956.

Holmes, Martin. *Shakespeare and His Players*. New York: Scribner, 1972.

Ingram, William. *The Business of Playing: The Beginnings of the Adult*

*Professional Theater in Elizabethan London*. Ithaca, N.Y.: Cornell University Press, 1992.

Lamb, Charles. *The Complete Works and Letters of Charles Lamb*. Edited by Saxe Commins. New York: Modern Library, 1935.

LeWinter, Oswald, ed. *Shakespeare in Europe*. Cleveland, Ohio: Meridian, 1963.

Marcus, Leah S. *Unediting the Renaissance: Shakespeare, Marlowe, Milton*. London: Routledge, 1996.

Orgel, Stephen. *The Authentic Shakespeare, and Other Problems of the Early Modern Stage*. New York: Routledge, 2002.

Salgado, Gamini. *Eyewitnesses of Shakespeare: First Hand Accounts of Performances, 1590–1890*. New York: Barnes and Noble, 1975.

Stern, Tiffany. *Rehearsal from Shakespeare to Sheridan.* Oxford: Clarendon Press, 2000.

Thomson, Peter. *Shakespeare's Professional Career.* Cambridge: Cambridge University Press, 1992.

Webster, Margaret. *Shakespeare without Tears.* New York: Whittlesey House, 1942.

Weimann, Robert. *Shakespeare and the Popular Tradition in the Theater: Studies in the Social Dimension of Dramatic Form and Function*. Edited by Robert Schwartz. Baltimore: Johns Hopkins University Press, 1978.

Wikander, Matthew H. *The Play of Truth and State: Historical Drama from Shakespeare to Brecht*. Baltimore: Johns Hopkins University Press, 1986.

Yachnin, Paul. *Stage-Wrights: Shakespeare, Jonson, Middleton, and the Making of Theatrical Value.* Philadelphia: University of Pennsylvania Press, 1997.

## Biography

Halliday, F. E. *The Life of Shakespeare.* Rev. ed. London: Duckworth, 1964.

Honigmann, F. A. J. *Shakespeare: The "Lost Years."* 2d ed. Manchester: Manchester University Press, 1998.

Schoenbaum, Samuel. *Shakespeare's Lives.* New ed. Oxford: Clarendon Press, 1991.

———. *William Shakespeare: A Compact Documentary Life.* Oxford: Oxford University Press, 1977.

## General

Bergeron, David M., and Geraldo U. de Sousa. *Shakespeare: A Study and Research Guide.* 3d ed. Lawrence: University of Kansas Press, 1995.

Berryman, John. *Berryman's Shakespeare.* Edited by John Haffenden. Preface by Robert Giroux. New York: Farrar, Straus and Giroux, 1999.

Bradbey, Anne, ed. *Shakespearian Criticism, 1919–35.* London: Oxford University Press, 1936.

Colie, Rosalie L. *Shakespeare's Living Art.* Princeton, N.J.: Princeton University Press, 1974.

Dean, Leonard F., ed. *Shakespeare: Modern Essays in Criticism.* Rev. ed. New York: Oxford University Press, 1967.

Goddard, Harold C. *The Meaning of Shakespeare.* 2 vols. Chicago: University of Chicago Press, 1951.

Kaufmann, Ralph J. *Elizabethan Drama: Modern Essays in Criticism.* New York: Oxford University Press, 1961.

McDonald, Russ. *The Bedford Companion to Shakespeare: An Introduction with Documents.* Boston: Bedford, 1996.

Raffel, Burton. *How to Read a Poem.* New York: Meridian, 1984.

Ricks, Christopher, ed. *English Drama to 1710.* Rev. ed. Harmondsworth: Sphere, 1987.

Siegel, Paul N., ed. *His Infinite Variety: Major Shakespearean Criticism Since Johnson.* Philadelphia: Lippincott, 1964.

Sweeting, Elizabeth J. *Early Tudor Criticism: Linguistic and Literary.* Oxford: Blackwell, 1940.

Van Doren, Mark. *Shakespeare.* New York: Holt, 1939.

# FINDING LIST

Repeated unfamiliar words and meanings, alphabetically arranged, with act, scene, and footnote number of first occurrence, in the spelling (form) of that first occurrence

| | | | |
|---|---|---|---|
| *advantage* | 1.3.49 | *cause* (noun) | 4.1.80 |
| *anon* | 2.2.72 | *chance* (verb) | 3.2.105 |
| *answer* (verb) | 3.5.20 | *charge* (noun) | 4.1.127 |
| *argosies* | 1.1.8 | *company* | 1.1.66 |
| *attend* | 1.1.74 | *conceit* | 1.1.100 |
| *bankrout* | 3.1.30 | *confound* | 3.2.176 |
| *bargains* | 1.3.33 | *conveniently* | 2.8.21 |
| *bated* | 1.3.102 | *cope* | 4.1.192 |
| *become* | 2.2.117 | *course* (noun) | 3.3.9 |
| *beshrew* | 2.6.41 | *curbed* | 1.2.27 |
| *bestow* | 2.2.81 | *dam* | 3.1.21 |
| *bids* (verb) | 2.2.7 | *delivered* | 3.3.7 |
| *bond* | 1.3.15 | *deny* | 2.2.113 |
| *by* (adverb) | 2.5.29 | *doubt, out of:* | |
| *carrion* | 2.7.41 | see under | |
| *casket* | 1.2.83 | *out of doubt* | |